T0115084

Dragon Lore Series

Legend of the Spirit Stone

Justin Snyder

authorHOUSE®

AuthorHouse™
1663 Liberty Drive
Bloomington, IN 47403
www.authorhouse.com
Phone: 1-800-839-8640

First published by AuthorHouse 3/28/2011

ISBN: 978-1-4567-5635-2 (sc)
ISBN: 978-1-4567-5634-5 (e)

Library of Congress Control Number: 2011904443

Printed in the United States of America

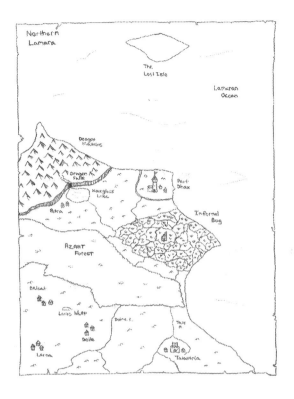

Game rules

This choose your own adventure series will require you to have a pencil, a d4, d6, d8, d10, and d20 dice. The d10 dice will be the most used dice in the game because it will be called the chance dice, its values will determine success in chance situations in the game. The other dice will determine damage in combat situations. This gaming novel will challenge its gamers to the best of their role playing abilities; careful thinking and strategy will be the only means of survival and book completion. The first step is to determine your attack rating, first you must roll the chance dice. This value is the base attack number, the next step to add 4 to the number plus whatever equipped weapon you possess. (Each weapon in this adventure has an attack bonus to be added to the base attack rating.) Example: You have just rolled a 6 on the chance dice, and your character has a dagger equipped and the attack bonus is 4. Your characters attack rating is now equal to 14. (If you enter combat without a weapon your attack rating returns to its base value. And the base damage you can inflict without a weapon is 1d4 damage.)

There are two weapon slots on the character sheet, one for each hand. You can only equip a maximum of two one handed weapons, and only one two- handed weapon, or a one-handed weapon and a shield. The next step is to determine your characters health points or (HP). First you must roll the chance dice and add twenty to the number. Example: You roll a 5 on the chance dice, your Health Point total will 25. This value is your characters life total if the number falls below one you are dead and the game is over. Your health point total cannot rise above its maximum total unless an item or magical effect allows you to do so. The third step in this process is to write down your magic point total, in this adventure you begin with **10** magic points. Magic points are used for casting your special abilities; the different spells cost different amounts of magic points. As the player you must decide on how best to use your magic points to succeed in your quest, and your magic point total cannot exceed 10 unless a magical ability or item allows you to do so.

The next step is to pick your special abilities, there are up to nine magical abilities to choose from. You may pick any 5 special abilities of the 9 to use on your quest. Choose carefully, picking the right abilities for use will aid you tremendously.

Special Abilities

1. Enhanced Senses

This unique ability does not cost its caster any magic points. Enhanced Senses enables the 5 senses to be pushed well beyond their normal range of sensitivity. You will become able to hear, smell, taste, see, and have your natural intuition increased three fold. If you choose Enhanced Senses, write it down on the character sheet.

2. Spirit - Fire

This special ability allows its user to channel their inner spiritual power into an offensive jet of searing flames; this ability can be used anytime in combat. The unique effect of this spell is that you are able to determine the magic point cost, for every 1 magic point spent using this ability it will deal 1d4 + 2 fire damage. If you choose Spirit- Fire, write it down on your character sheet.

3. Elementalism

This power allows the caster complete dominion over the four elements, wind, water, fire, and granite. Every element has its own advantages and disadvantages, but when in desperation the forces of the elemental plain can aid in ways that you would never expect. The cost of using this spell per use is 2 magic points. If you choose Elementalism, write it down on your character sheet.

4. Herbalism

The use of this skill does not cost any magic points, and you gain total knowledge of potion mixing and herbs, as well as how to use volatile chemicals. You will be required to use empty vials for potion storing and a pestle and mortar for mixing the potions correctly. If you choose Herbalism, write it down on your character sheet. (If chosen you automatically gain the pestle and mortar, an herb pouch with 6 slots, as well as 3 empty vials.)

5. <u>Tolerance</u>

In dire situations where death is eminent, and you need a saving grace this is the skill for you. Your body can push itself beyond its normal threshold, and you can withstand situations that could normally kill you. There is no set magic point cost for this skill; the cost will differ with each use. Sometimes the price to stave off death is worth the cost. If you choose Tolerance, write it down on your character sheet.

6. <u>Necromancy</u>

Perhaps the most powerful of magical skills, but also the most unpredictable. Necromancy permits its user with command over the dead, and the ability to communicate with the spirit world. But with the short cut to power, there can be a high price to pay. The initial cost for use of this spell costs 4 magic points. If you choose Necromancy, write it down on your character sheet.

7. <u>Curing</u>

This ability allows the user to heal wounds with unnatural means of recovery. This skill can be used in direct combat, as well as any time in the game. The cost for using this spell costs 2 magic points, and heals 6 health points (HP). If you choose Curing, write it down on your character sheet.

8. <u>Invisibility</u>

This powerful ability allows the caster to slip into the blind spots of others, a trick of the mind that can allow you to pass by your enemies undetected for a very brief period of time. The use of this skill costs 3 magic points. If you choose Invisibility, write it down on your character sheet.

9. <u>Fore-sight</u>

This ability will permit is caster the ability to see glimpses into the past, or future. This can be useful for detecting events and outcomes in the near future. The user is also able to deduce clues and knowledge about puzzles just by touching objects. The cost for using this unique ability is 2 magic points. If you choose Fore-Sight, write it down on your character sheet.

Equipment

Equipment comes in a variety of forms, such as weapons, food rations, and etc. All of these items except for equipped weapons are kept in the backpack. There are a total of 10 slots for backpack items, most items take up only one slot. Larger items can take up to two or more slots, depending on what that item is. You begin with four meals and three empty vials in your backpack. There is also a separate section which will represent your pockets called the special items pouch. There are four slots for special items, for things such as rings, amulets, scrolls, parchments, and etc. Below this paragraph are the list of weapons and the bonuses as well as damage that each will provide. (Roll the chance dice to determine your starting weapon.)

1- <u>Dagger</u> - One-handed- Attack value- 4 (Damage: 1d4)

2 -<u>Rapier </u>- One-handed- Attack value -5 (Damage: 1d4+1)

3 -<u>Mace</u> -One-handed- Attack value -6 (Damage: 1d4+2)

4 -<u>Axe</u> - One-handed -Attack value- 6 (Damage: 1d4+3)

5- <u>War hammer </u>- One-handed -Attack value -7 (Damage: 1d6+1)

6 -<u>Sword</u> -One-handed- Attack value -8 (Damage: 1d6+2)

7 -<u>Staff</u> -Two-handed - Attack value- 7 (Damage: 1d6) (Adds one extra point of damage to spirit- fire)

8 -<u>Large Axe</u> -Two-handed -Attack value -9 (Damage: 1d6+ 4)

9- <u>Broadsword</u> -Two- handed - Attack value-10 (Damage: 1d8+3)

0 -<u>Spear</u> -Two-handed -Attack value-11 (Damage: 1d8+4)

*- <u>Bow</u> -Two-handed - Attack value- 8 (Damage: 1d8)

*- <u>Cross-Bow</u> - Two-handed -Attack value-12 (Damage: 1d8+4)

*- <u>Pole-Axe</u> -Two-handed- Attack value -13 (Damage: 1d10+3)

Shields

Shields take up one slot of the two on your weapons section of the character sheet, and you are not able to carry a two handed weapon when you have a shield equipped. Shields can be useful in combat, and reduce damage taken in combat and block missile type attacks. This is a list of all the shields that exist in this game series.

1 - <u>Wooden shield</u> - armor class-1- reduces combat damage by 1 point.

2 - <u>Buckler</u> -armor class -1- reduces combat damage by 2 points.

3 - <u>Large shield</u> -armor class-2- reduces combat damage by 2 points.

4 -<u>Tower shield</u> - armor class-2- reduces combat damage by 3 points.

Armor Class

Armor class is a level represented for combat use for your characters defense status, this is the number that will determine a hit or miss in the combat. The higher this value is the better chance that you have of the enemy missing your character in combat. For every garment of clothing and armor that your character has equipped adds one point to the armor class value. Example: Sabin is wearing his cloak, a pair of boots, and a wooden shield so the armor class value would be 3. (Sabin's armor class cannot exceed 10 points, unless a spell or magical item permits it to do so.) You begin this game with an armor class of 1. When the armor class is reduced below zero that is how much damage will be added to the attack when the character is struck. Example: Sabin is in combat with a warlock and the warlock has reduced his armor class by 4 points from a spell, resulting in the armor class being -3. Next the warlock deals a total of 6 damage, but because of the negative value he not only hits Sabin but instead of dealing a total of 6 damage Sabin is dealt 9 damage.

Special Items

There are a maximum of four slots for special items, special items include things like rings, amulets, parchments, and the like. Things of great importance are placed here, and each takes up one slot unless the book states otherwise.

Support and Potions

Along with the aid of Herbalism, there are also potions of various kinds that can do any number of things such as heal wounds, raise combat status, and inflict heavy damage on enemies. If you do not posses the ability Curing, but you have Herbalism then potions become a must in game strategy. The most basic potions will be listed below.

1. Green moss potion - Restores 4 health points.

2. Red moss potion - Deals 1d6+3 fire damage to an enemy.

3. Antidote - Cures poison, blindness, almost every form status ailment there is.

4. Elixir - restores 4 magic points.

Health Points (HP)	Magic Points	ATTACK :
		Base attack :
0° Dead		Armor class :

| Damage : | Coin Purse | Quiver : |
| | MAX: 100 copper | |

Weapons / Armor	ATK (AC)	DMG /~ Dmg / effects
1		
2		

Armor	(AC)	~ DMG / EFFECTS
1		
2		
3		
4		

Herbalism Pouch

1
2
3
4
5
6

Back Pack

1
2
3
4
5
6
7
8
9
10

Special Items

1
2
3
4

Rules for combat

There will be many situations during the course of the role playing adventure that you will have to fight an enemy in combat. The enemy will have their own set of Attack rating, Health points, Armor class, and if they have magical abilities their own set of points as well. Some monsters also have immunities and resistances, and those will be listed following the enemy status. (Do not forget that if you enter combat without a weapon, your attack rating will be its base value and not have the attack bonus granted by having an equipped weapon.)   The sequence for combat is as follows.

1. Add all bonus's for your Attack and subtract that number from the enemy's armor class to obtain the hit/miss ratio.

2. Next you must roll the d20 dice and roll below the hit/miss ratio to successfully hit the enemy, and the same rules apply for the enemy striking Sabin. (Sabin always gets the first chance to strike unless combat dictates otherwise.) Example: Sabin is in combat with a Bandit. Sabin's attack rating is 12 currently, and the Bandit's armor class is 3. The hit/miss ratio is 9, and a 9 or lower must be rolled for Sabin to hit the Bandit. (Also if a 1 is rolled with the d20 it is considered a critical strike, in which a vulnerable area on the enemy is hit and the damage dealt is doubled! And the same rule is applied on the enemy end of the hit/miss roll. Remember you must always roll the dice for the hit/miss ratio even if the number exceeds 20, because 1 always represents a critical hit and 20 is always a miss!)

3. If you have hit the enemy then roll your damage dice, and apply any extra damage as necessary. If Sabin does not roll high enough to hit the enemy, then the enemy gets its chance to attack.

4. You also have the option to use any spells, such as Spirit-Fire for extra damage. Or any offensive potions, and support potions needed to win the combat.

5. Do not forget to subtract or add any damage done to Sabin or the enemy by either a negative hit/miss ratio, or if a shield is equipped by either party.

6. Repeat steps 1-5 until the enemy's health point total reaches zero, or Sabin's does first.

The Story so far

In the wondrous world of Lamara, there is a small village beside the dangerously enchanted Azart Forest called Lorna. The inhabitants are the descendants of an ancient clan of mages that guard the sacred spirit stone, a mysterious but dangerous vessel of creation and destruction. Entrusted by the Elf's, the high race and guardians of life the villagers of Lorna pass the gift of magic on through they're children to continue to protect the spirit stone and uphold the balance of existence. But unknown to the pristine world of Lamara a dark force is coming, something evil begins to wash over the elements of fantasy and magic in search of the most valuable artifact in existence. You are but an eager naive young apprentice to the Lorna guild mage, being trained to understand balance and take his place as protector of the spirit stone. Your day begins as any other, and you begin your quest finishing your weekly hunt in the outskirts of the village. Only you can determine the course of events that will ensue by turning to section **1**.

1

It is a warm summer day along the Lorna grasslands, the bright orange and yellow sun beams down on you intensely as you finish your midday hunt. After resetting a snare from the day before you have managed to capture a rabbit, the small white furry rodent desperately tries to free itself from your trap but to no avail. Quickly and as painlessly as possible you end the small rabbit's life, and after gutting the evenings supper you pack it away in your backpack. (There is enough of the kill for two meals, mark this on your character sheet.) Now you are on your way back home with your bounty and a wide satisfied smile on your young face. You are also excited about the next coming day as you will be finishing your apprenticeship with the village guild mage; it is seen as a great honor to become a mage.

The once loud noises of birds chirping have suddenly stopped and a wave of cold dread runs down your spine. You dash to the top of the nearest hill that overlooks your home you notice an alarming sight. Plumes of black smoke are spewing into the clear sky, and roaring red-orange flames are devouring the housing of your village. Sorrow and confusion overwhelm your senses as you try to figure out what is happening and why?

If you possess the special ability Fore-Sight and wish to use it turn to **150.**

Or if you do not possess this ability or do not wish to use it and would rather run closer to the burning sight and investigate turn to **240.**

2

You bend down and examine the clusters of herbs that are growing beside the trail, immediately identify it as hood grass. When ground down into a watery green liquid with your pestle and mortar you can craft elixir potions. (There are enough hood grass plants to make up to 3 elixir potions that can restore up to 4 magic points, remember you cannot raise your magic point total past 10.) You also notice cinder mushrooms growing next to the hood grass. You can use the dark red orange mushroom caps to make incendiary potions just by grinding the caps into a powder and placing them inside empty vials. (There are enough mushroom caps to make up to 3 incendiary potions that deal 1d12 +4 fire damage each. However when the potions are used you cannot reclaim the empty vials back for use.) After you have finished mixing and crafting any number of potions you wish to use and store, remember to adjust your character sheet accordingly.

Turn to **60.**

3

The remainder of your day is uneventful and danger does not seem to be evident, your trek has been relaxing and peaceful. You regain **2** health points, as night approaches the full moon lights your way enough that you do not need to light a torch. Shadows dance around in all directions and different noises as well as howling chill you to your core. One could truly go mad in such an immense forest, especially one with such mysterious magical forces. You notice a patch of wild strawberries growing just ahead, after you survey the area for any danger you taste one of the sweet juicy berries. (You may take two meals worth of strawberries.) After you have had your fill, you continue on your way to search for a suitable campsite to rest for the night. After a few moments you notice the entrance to a clearing ahead, hoping that you are entering Allendrah you hurriedly approach the clearing but your surprise you notice that it is an old graveyard of some sort. Tombstones line the barren field sized clearing, and in the distance you can make out the shape of an old crypt.

If you wish to explore the graveyard and crypt turn to **70.**

Or if you would rather ignore the graveyard and continue searching for a campsite turn to **112.**

If you possess the special ability Fore- Sight and wish to use it before making a decision turn to **172.**

ч

Nightfall comes quickly, succumbing to the effects of an exhausting day you do not hesitate to make camp. You must eat one meal or lose **4** health points. Immediately after your meal you drift into a long deep sleep, and when you awaken the following morning you restore **3** health points and **1** magic point. The morning proves to be a new challenge as it begins to rain, after just moments you are drenched and the trail begins to get extremely muddy and difficult to traverse. The thick sticky heavy mud almost consumes your entire boots with every slow step you take; the water falling from the sky is matting your clothing to your skin and making your body feel heavier and more sluggish. To make things even worse the trail suddenly stops just a few feet ahead, you stop and look around for signs of any other trails or markers but to your extreme disappointment and confusion there are none. Bewildered by the sudden end of the trail, you scratch your head and ponder a solution.

If you possess the guardian ring, turn to 80.

If you do not possess this magical item and possess the special ability Fore-Sight and wish to use it turn to **110.**

If you do not possess this special ability and would rather use Enhanced Senses turn to **135.**

If you do not possess either of these abilities or the guardian ring turn to **236.**

5

The monstrous bear growls one last time before crashing to the ground dead and lifeless, you sigh with relief and take a moment to rest before you get your bearings straightened out again. Night soon approaches; you must eat a meal or lose **4** health points. You decide not to fall asleep so quickly because of the noises and movement all around you; unsure of why there is more night activity than usual you wait to sleep until it quiets down a little. You awaken the following morning refreshed, you regain **3** health points. You begin to wonder how much longer you can take surviving and traveling this treacherous place? You pray that Allendrah is close and your journey will soon come to a close. The sun never breaks through the forest canopy today, and that sets a grim nervous mood for you as you travel. The shadows of the trees dance around tauntingly, and the bird chirping soon comes to a dead silence. The tiny hairs on the back of your neck begin to stand up, and your heart pounds loudly in your chest as you approach a wall of briar patch that stretches as far as the eye can see and well over the trees. You stare at the strange overgrowth with confusion until you spot a single opening just ahead. Like the mouth of a dark cave it beckons to you, shrugging your shoulders you walk over towards the opening. Realizing that this briar growth covers everything ahead this opening is the only way to precede ahead. Nervously you enter the small mouth of the cave, careful not to get pricked by the thorns of the plant. The floor of what appears to be a tunnel is solid rock, dirt, and thick damp moss. It soon becomes dark like in a cave, (you must use stick and **1** magic point to create a spark to light your way unless you have a torch to spare.) After you have walked several more feet the tunnel forks into three different paths.

If you possess the ability of Fore-Sight and wish to use it turn to **45.**

If you do not possess this ability and would rather use Enhanced- Senses turn to **94.**

If you do not possess either of these abilities, but you have the Guardian ring, turn to **109.**

If you do not possess the guardian ring and would like to take the tunnel leading left turn to **123.**

If you choose to the take the tunnel leading right turn to **161.**

If you would prefer to take the tunnel straight ahead turn to **205.**

6

You force your body to move around the bandits that attempt to stop you; fortunately you are quick enough to avoid capture. They shout amongst themselves in frustration in their inability to capture one person. Soon you have managed to put a great amount of distance between yourself and your pursuers, you can hear them shouting. "We got one trying to run Lord Falco!" Shouts one of the bandits in the distance behind you. You glance back to notice that the bandit leader is among his men with a longbow and already has an arrow notched and ready to fire.

If you possess a shield and wish to use it turn to **78.**

If you do not or do not wish to use it instead roll the chance dice.

If you rolled 0-4, turn to **134.**

If you rolled 5 or higher turn to **203.**

7

You are not quick enough to escape the path of a strange green fluid that is being secreted from the large spider's maw, the second the green substance touches you there is an intense burning sensation that forces you to scream out in pain. Your face, throat, and chest are rapidly being dissolved by very potent acidic saliva. You attempt to wipe off the fluid, but you end up burning your hands and spreading it. You are now writhing and screaming on the floor just as the briar arachnid closes in for its kill. The last thing you see before an agonizing death is the sharp saw like arm of the spider slicing you down your middle.

Your life and quest end here!

8

You try to run away from the range of the mysterious cloud, but you only make it several feet before the effects of the gas start to slow your movements down. Desperately you fight the symptoms of the gas, but movement becomes more and more difficult.

If you possess an antidote potion turn to **212.**
If you do not possess an antidote potion, but possess the special ability curing turn to **275.**
If you do not possess an antidote potion, or the ability of curing you must quickly draw your weapon and attempt to kill the mushrooms by turning to **87.**

9

As soon as you turn the rusty dial to the numeral nine, there is a loud click and you can hear the internal mechanism of the lock open the stone door slowly. It grates loudly as the door shifts to the left opening the entrance to the crypt, immediately the smell of mold and death hits you and you step back coughing loudly. After the dust cloud parts you cautiously step inside the chamber, it is dark so dark that you cannot see anything in front of you. (If you do not possess a torch you must use **1** magic point to create a light source.) The chamber is large and the stone floor is covered in dust and cobwebs, the walls have ancient engravings and pictographs all over. What immediately grabs your attention are two sarcophagi in the center of the chamber, one has a red cover on it and the other has a green cover on it. You walk over towards the red sarcophagus; you realize that the Riven mage buried here was named: Ulzar Bezarias, a legend among your order. And the second sarcophagus bears the body of: Elaine Mertide, the most famous Riven sorceress that ever lived. You do not recall any back history of these two; you are only familiar with the names and titles that both of these legendary Riven clan members had. But you begin to notice that they markings below their names are a puzzle.

Keepers of the ancient secret are we
Any who embark on our legendary history must prove themselves as true Riven Magi
Only the power of ones spirit can invoke entry to the next room.

You pause as you ponder the solution to the ancient riddle, and you realize that you must use your own magical abilities to activate whatever force will allow you to proceed.

If you choose the power of Necromancy turn to **77.**

If you choose the power of Elementalism instead turn to **137.**

If you choose the ability Spirit-Fire turn to **228.**

10

You take a deep breath before leaving the safety of the trail; the terrain proves more difficult to pass than you hoped. Bushes and thorns scrape your face and arms as you continue in the direction that the trail was heading, your cloths also become torn and ripped. Take 1d4 damage from the thorn bushes that surround the area. After walking a few hundred feet you decide to re-locate the trail, you head back in the direction that the trail should be in. You suddenly realize that you cannot find the trail, confused by how you could so easily become lost you feel panic setting in. Desperately you back track slightly and try to follow your footprints back to the trail, after a few minutes your prints have vanished. You curse your unfortunate luck, you must find the trail or you will never find Allendrah. Roll the chance dice.

If you rolled 0-4 turn to **165.**
If you rolled 5 or higher turn to **276.**

11

You turn around and hurriedly back track to the fork, and without taking extra time to think about which of three tunnels to take your instincts steer you into the closest tunnel. You can no longer hear any clicking noises which brings you a little relief, and after a short time the tunnel begins to slope downward. The air becomes more humid and musky, sweat pours from your face. It is dark, enough so that if you do not possess a torch you must expend **1** magic to create a light source. Soon you step into a large chamber; it is circular with only one way out. But the most peculiar feature of this chamber is the walls are covered with large white pulsating sacs.

You are not sure who or what has placed these here? But they are fused to the vines and briars of the wall by a strange webbing of some sort? Your curiosity overwhelms you as you raise your light source closer to the sacs; you can see the shapes moving around inside. Some kind of bug or bugs are inside, each about the size of your hand. You step back in surprise and disgust, and your presence has also stirred activity inside all of the sacs as they pulsate violently. You shudder in detest as the sacs start to rip open revealing dozens of palm sized spider like creatures, they are bright green with only one eye in the center of their heads. They make shrill squealing noises as they pour from their egg sacs and in a single coordinated wave charge towards you.

If you wish to flee from this brood chamber turn to **289.**

If you would rather stay and fight off these spiders turn to **321.**

12

You very slowly begin to creep closer and closer to the bandits, they do not seem to notice your slow advance but the horses they are on begin to grow nervous and begin to snort and stomp their hoofs loudly. The bandits suddenly become alert and begin to study their surroundings. You must roll the chance dice.

If you rolled 0-4 turn to **178.**
If you rolled 5 or higher turn to **227.**

Just walking is making your legs burn with exhaustion and the uphill climb does not appeal to your liking either. As you climb the mountain of lose mud and forest debris you notice what appears to be something standing at the top. The silhouette is almost man like, and you freeze in your steps not sure if it is a bandit or something else unfriendly. Cautiously you observe the motionless figure that continues to stand there, and then when your nerves slacken you continue to climb. When you finally reach the top of the hill like terrain, you notice that the figure is actually some kind of statue. The stone is light gray, covered in green moss, and very weathered. The statue appears to be a short gnome about five feet tall, it has a large cap; also the statue is in a strange position. Its left arm points in one direction and the arm points to the ground, and there also a stone tablet by the base of its feet. A closer look reveals an inscription on the tablet that reads:

**All who wander the forest have yet to
find the true path
Ye who venture too far lose sight of the trail
To find ones destination note the six fingers of the
black tree
Listen to the wind of the hollows
And ye shall come upon the owl's second eye.
and true path**.

It is obvious that this riddle is some sort of clue on how to find your way past the glamour of the forest and locate the correct trail, (Remember that the clue involves the numbers **6** and **2**.) You figured out that you are so off course that someone or something has put this here to help any who are lost a way out. You take a moment to figure out the mystery of this riddle and figure the clue to solving it has to do with the numbers mentioned.

If you have solved the mystery of the riddle turn to the section number of the result.

If you are unable to solve this puzzle turn to **268.**

14

After you have slain the entire brood, you waste no time to vacate the chamber and continue along the tunnel. It winds and turns abruptly making it difficult to trek and prepare for any surprises, but you always slow down around a corner to make sure that there isn't a hidden threat lurking nearby. After traveling another mile or so undisturbed, you arrive at another fork in the tunnel. There are two paths before you, a tunnel leading straight upward, and then a tunnel leading to the left.

If you wish to take the tunnel leading upward turn to **202.**

If you would rather take the tunnel going in the left direction turn to **131.**

15

After your nerves are completely calmed and you are focused, you use all of your senses to determine what the best route for you to travel is. You shudder as a grim sensation runs down your spine; overwhelming dread has flooded your body. You sense extreme danger in the left path, to what detail you are not sure. But you know that your instincts would not betray you, death awaits you in the left path.

If you wish to take the right path turn to **307.**

If you do not trust your instincts and wish to take the left path turn to **237.**

16

In your attempt to outrun the enraged large bear you are struck in the back by its large paws, you roll on the ground and fight to gain your footing back. The bear is upon you, its heavy body is crushing you as its large head slams into your chest the wind is knocked from your lungs. Dazed you are unable to recover fully you feel its mouth around your head, you attempt to escape but you are unable to move. The bear's teeth pierce your skin and its jaw feels like a vice around your head, death comes quickly as it crushes your head in its jaws like a thin eggshell.

Your life and quest end here.

17

You are prepared to face these large spiders, but you are soon unsure when you see how many approach you. Four of these arachnid's jump in front of you, they hiss and click at you wildly as they prepare they're attack. You hold your ground realizing that there is no way out of this fight now, and suddenly three of the spiders leap into the air.

3 Briar Arachnids

Attack. 24   **Health points. 34**
Armor class. 3   **Magic points. 0**

Hit: 1d12 +2

(These creatures are weak to fire, incendiary potions and spirit-fire damage is doubled!)

If you survive the combat turn to **107**.

18

You leave the inn behind and decide to explore the surrounding area, perhaps a farmer or someone here would have directions to find the Azart Forest. When you walk into the marketplace you are presented with many resources that could provide the information you seek. You notice a tavern, an herbalist shop, and a smithy.

If you wish to enter the tavern turn to **58.**

Or if the herbalist shop holds your interest turn to **102.**

Or if you would prefer to seek information in the smithy turn to **208.**

19

With the expense of **1** magic point you aim your extended palm at the large strange briar arachnid, and a hissing jet of white spirit-fire leaps from your hand and engulfs the creature. It screams and hisses loudly as it leaps back forth trying to put the flames that it is covered in out, but it is already dead before you pass the burning body. You stare at the smoking remains of the large spider for a moment, then the hairs on your neck stand up when you glance down the tunnel behind you and can a horde of briar arachnids advancing, there are too many to count. You force your body to move towards the exit, you must find safety and quickly.

There are far too many of these spiders to fight off, there must be over a hundred. It is a flood of spiders that are determined to destroy you. The hissing, shrieking, and clicking noises are so loud and many that your ears begin to ring as you force yourself to the end of the tunnel, it seems like you are running in slow motion towards your goal. When you finally set foot outside the exit tunnel of this massive nest you are relieved to be back in the outdoors of this forest, the fresh air and feel of the suns light on your skin brings instant relief. But that joy will be short lived if you do not find high ground immediately.

Turn to **187.**

20

Carefully you extend an open palm at your target and at the cost of **1** magic point you let a single jet of white hissing flames loose. The troll is ultimately alarmed by the attack, and even more surprised by the effectiveness of the magic. The troll is covered in the fire and screaming in pain as the fire consumes and burns its hideous flesh. The other troll noticing its comrade's pain grows weary of attacking you. Instead of continuing its pursuit, the troll growls at you as you flee. After you are completely winded do you stop and look over your shoulders, you sigh when you notice that you are not being followed.

Turn to **3.**

21

You take your right hand and aim it behind you at one of the bandit horsemen, and at the cost of **1** magic point you release a white jet of searing flames that roll onto one of the horsemen. The man screams in pain, and falls from his steed, and the bandits steed runs right into the other bandit rider next to it and the other bandit is sent flying backwards from his stallion. Falco does not stop or show any signs of fear from your surprise attack, he steers his black horse around his wounded fallen men and continues to pursue you. Soon his horse is on you, the shape of the large bandit leader appears right next to you. Falco draws his weapon and attacks. (This fight will only last two rounds.)

Falco Drifkan (Bandit leader)

Attack. 24   **Health points. 28**
Armor Class. 4   **Magic points. 0**

Hit: 1d6 +3

If you survive the two rounds of combat turn to **194.**

22

You prepare as best you can for such an attack, but due to your inability to maneuver properly because of the deep sticky mud covering the tunnel floor you must deduct **2** points from your attack.

2 Briar Arachnids

Attack. 20   **Health points. 26**

Armor class. 2   **Magic points. 0**

Hit: 1d8 +2

(Remember these creatures are weak to fire, incendiary potions and spirit-fire damage is doubled.)

If you survive the combat turn to **209.**

23

You take this opportunity to run before the burning troll is able to recover, and make a clean escape. You continually glance over your shoulder to make sure that you are not being followed, but when you notice that you are not being chased you stop to catch your breath. After you have recovered enough to continue your quest, you take a moment to get your sense of direction and continue west.

Turn to **3.**

24

Holding the spirit stone in your palm you concentrate on creating spirit-fire, a warm tingling sensation fills your arm and runs all over your body. A sense of peace and clear mindedness takes over you as the white fire from your palm surrounds the small rock. Suddenly the stone trembles slightly and it lights up like a bright vibrant beacon of hope, it is like a solar eclipse you are forced to shield eyes from the blinding light that illuminates the entire forest. A gentle breeze flows around you, and the spider horde pauses screeching and hisses as the light blinds them. You can feel a surge of power unlike any other flowing freely through you, the wisdom and history of the Riven magi is now one with you completely. You feel pride as you finally have managed to re-light the stone and activate its powers once again, now you can find Allendrah.

Next like a tidal wave of energy the spirit stone blasts a thick white searing beam into the sky, and then the beams split into smaller rays of spirit-fire jets that singe and fry every single briar arachnid that is surrounding you. The sound of screeching and clicking grows louder than the hissing of the hundreds of spirit-fire bolts that are shot from the stone. You have never seen or could even comprehend such power, and you are astonished that you are behind it. Soon the spirit stones light grow dimmer as it stops firing streams of white fire; every single briar arachnid has been slain. There are hundreds of blackened ball shaped corpses before you. The stone radiates a warm soothing aura around you as you hold it tightly in your hands, (Restore any lost health points and magic points to their original level.) As you prepare to set off something new catches your eyes.

Turn to **241.**

25

You very cautiously tip toe and slither from bush to bush without incident, as you enter the alleyway you can hear the screams and cries of pain from the other villagers that are being held captive. Just when you think that you are in the clear, suddenly one of the broad shouldered men appears in front of you will a grin on his dirty weathered face? "Another survivor!" He growls as he draws a curved sword from his sheath.

If you wish to attack this man turn, to **270**.
Or if you would rather flee turn to **342.**

26

With the cost of another magic point, you quickly fire another deadly stream of white fire onto your enemy. The fiery attack consumes the arachnid before it can reach you and it dies quickly at your feet. You with relief, and take a deep breath before continuing your trek.

Turn to **61.**

27

Carefully you press onward avoiding the pulsating sacs that are on the walls, the deeper you manage to get, the thicker the mud becomes and the warmer the air is. Wiping your forehead free of the perspiration that is now covering your body, you begin to hear strange clicking noises. You freeze in your steps and try to hear and locate where the strange clicks are coming from, but to your dismay you are unable to tell which direction they are coming from.

If you possess the ability Enhanced-Senses and wish to use them turn to **73.**

If you do not possess this ability and instead would like to use Fore-Sight turn to **140.**

If you do not possess either of these abilities or do not wish to use them turn to **199.**

28

You turn around and follow the trail back the way you came, you look past the trees ahead and wonder if you can just go around the mushroom circles. You step off the trail and proceed ahead in hopes that the strange mushrooms are only in the vicinity ahead by the trail. To your dismay after several minutes of walking you find that the mushrooms cover the entire area, and grow in thicker clusters off the trail. Scratching your head you walk back towards the trail, it does take a little while to find the trail again.

If you wish to back track even farther and perhaps locate a different trail to proceed on turn to **114.**

Or if you would rather just continue on the trail and pass through the toadstool rings turn to **297.**

29

The second the green fluid hits your body it splashes all over your face and down your throat and chest, immediately a burning sensation makes you scream in agony and drop to the ground. Apparently these creatures can secrete an acidic fluid that can melt anything, you quickly attempt to wipe off the blazing fluid, but that only makes it worse and spreads it. Soon you are peeling off your own skin, and you are unable to breath. Before you can die a slow painful death, you are hacked to pieces by the spider attacker.

Tragically, your life and quest end here!

30

You stand ready as the massive beast charges up to you for battle, its size alone is intimidating but you must now fight to the death.

Large bear

Attack. 18   **Health points. 30**
Armor class. 3   **Magic points. 0**

Hit: 1d6 +5

If you survive the combat turn to **5.**

31

You run to the nearest building and crouch around the corner and peek over in the distance, you bite your lip nervously when you see two bandits setting fire to the neighboring buildings. The other villagers are growing restless and terrified, you also notice that there are four villagers to every bandit that has muscled they're way in. Perhaps if you set the stage for the villagers using their numbers to overcome this foe you can make your escape. One of your special abilities would suffice for such a task.

If you wish to use the ability Elementalism, turn to 143.

Or if you would prefer to use Spirit-Fire turn to **223.**

If you do not possess either of these abilities or do not wish to use them and would rather use the ability of Invisibility for means of escape turn to **266.**

If you do not possess the ability Invisibility and would rather run for it turn to **335.**

32

The arachnid duo is upon you quickly, they simultaneously swing they're slashing saw like arms at you. You dodge the first series of attacks, and manage to hold your ground. You cannot evade this combat.

2 Briar Arachnids

Attack. 20	**Health points. 26**
Armor class. 2	**Magic points. 0**

Hit: 1d8 +3

(Remember these creatures are weak to fire, incendiary potions and spirit-fire damage is doubled.)

After you have slain your attackers, continue by turning to **61.**

33

Your five enhanced senses detect an unknown danger lurking in the left tunnel, but you are unable to pick anything up with your senses for the other tunnel. You detect a faint odor that is new to your senses; it is a sweet but musky odor that makes your nostrils twitch. The odor is coming from the left tunnel, and you assume that the strange smell has something do with the danger that you sense down that tunnel.

If you wish to take the left tunnel turn to **238.**
If you choose the right tunnel instead turn to **329.**

34

You can feel a field of magic emanating around you that you have never felt before, you can tell that is very old and powerful. One of the elf sayings is that the forest is alive, and to underestimate its power is to truly be a fool. This forest contains very ancient magical properties that you are not remotely familiar with, and your entire body tingles from the magic. You realize that you are lucky to have made it this far, rumors are well known that no one in the past century has survived in the Azart Forest for more than two days. You freeze in your steps when you suddenly hear the loud noise of what you think is a branch snapping in two. You slowly turn and look around with your eyes to see what and where the noise came from, but you do not see anything out of the ordinary. Just as you begin to calm down and continue on your way, the peace and quiet is disturbed by a loud rustling noise just ahead of you. Blinking your eyes in disbelief you rub them roughly, and look upon the movement in the distance. To your surprise it appears as if the forest moving, tree branches are swaying in unnatural positions and the sound of loud stomping echoes loudly in your mind as the largest and nearest is walking towards you. Terror and nervousness are your immediate reaction, but whether it is friendly or hostile is a complete mystery?

If you wish to approach the walking tree, turn to 230.

If you would rather attack the strange being, turn to **304.**

35

The left tunnel proves to be more sinister looking than you had hoped the air is so musky and humid you sweat profusely and this slows your pace dramatically. Just when you think it couldn't get any worse inside this insidious labyrinth, you see two briar arachnids directly ahead of you. These two are different then the others they are both jet black and have oversized saw like forearms. The second they notice you they immediately spring into action with a series of loud hissing noises then they charge directly at you.

If you have a bow or crossbow and wish to use it turn to **181.**

If you do not have a bow or any projectile weapon, but possess the ability spirit-fire and wish to use it turn to **226.**

If you do not possess a bow or the ability spirit-fire, turn to **299.**

36

After a few more hours the sun begins to set over the vast beautiful Lorna grasslands, you realize that you are starving. (You must eat one meal or lose 4 health points.) You know that if you keep walking east that you will find the Azart Forest, and you dread the danger that lurks inside the expansive wilderness. You have never been there before, but you remember the stories of all kinds of monsters that wander the forest. You find a safe location to set a campfire and rest for the night; it is surprisingly quiet out here at night. Whenever you have ventured here to hunt rabbits, the plains have always been very active with birds, gophers, rabbits, and a myriad of insects. You remove the spirit stone from your backpack; it is cold and still looks like an ordinary rock in appearance. You must activate its power again to find Allendrah, you recall your mentor telling you that it is the key to completing your quest. After you place the rock back into your backpack your eye lids begin to feel very heavy and you can no longer stave off the effects of exhaustion and sleep.

Turn to **122.**

37

The small pixies flutter around you intrusively as you patiently wait to see what they are going to do, whispering fills your ears and mind but you cannot make out what they are saying. The spirit stones aura seems to attract more of these ferries towards you, "How came you by this stone?" One of the small sprites asks in a high voice. The ferry appears in front of your face, he has long amber colored hair and yellow eyes that pierce into you. You explain that to the fae that surround you that it came into your charge by your mentor and last carrier of the relic. You also add that you are trying to return it to the elves of Allendrah and that you desire their aid to find it. The cloud of sprites do not seem persuaded by your story, "Our queen is the only one of us that can guide you to your destination, but only by uttering her sacred name will earn you such a request." Whispers the tiny ferry. You frown as you attempt to recall the name of the ferry queen, but you have no idea of what her secret name is?

If you wish to answer, "Oona." As the name turn to **43.**

If you choose to answer, "Zfehndell." As the name turn to **69.**

If you would rather answer, "Alleriah." As the name turn to **84.**

If you think the answer is, "Tameriah." Turn to **129.**

If you possess the special ability of Fore-sight and wish to use it to obtain the answer turn to **239.**

38

You have your weapon ready as the large beast growls at you then leaps for your throat, you cannot evade this fight it will be to the death.

Large wolf

Attack. 10   **Health points. 14**

Armor class. 1   **Magic points. 0**

Hit: 1d6 +1

After the wolf is slain, four more large wolves suddenly appear in proximity of you. The slaying of their kin has not deterred their insatiable appetite for your flesh, fighting off one wolf was not a problem but you doubt that you can handle four more at once.

If you wish to attempt to flee the wolves turn to **97.**
If you would rather stand your ground and fight these fearsome hungry animals turn to **128.**

39

You manage to have your weapon ready as the two large soldier briar arachnids advance, they hiss and make clicking noises as they charge. You cannot evade this fight; you are in the point of no return.

2 Soldier Briar Arachnids

Attack. 26   **Health points. 30**
Armor class. 2   **Magic points. 0**

Hit: 1d12 +3

(Remember these creatures are weak to fire, incendiary potions and spirit-fire damage is doubled.)
If you survive the combat turn to **63.**

40

Your ears become filled with the most horrible howl that you have ever heard, fear and panic fill your body as you can hear growling around you and breathing. Your eyes dart in all directions as you try to lock onto whatever is sneaking around you. You can only see bushes moving and shadows darting around the nearby trees. You stand ready for any threat that is going to produce itself; you jump back in alarm when a large grizzled wolf jumps out in front of you. It has long gray and black hair, yellow eyes, white gleaming long fangs, and is larger than any wolf you have ever seen. It growls furiously as it creeps closer and closer towards you.

If you wish to run from the wolf turn to **182.**
If you would rather attack this beast, turn to **220.**

41

The tunnel leading upward proves to be an easy route, and one that renews your hopes of escaping this awful place. You can see sunlight poking through the ceiling of the tunnel, and feel the freeze cool air of the outside. You soon realize that this tunnel leads to an exit; joy soon follows your renewed hopes. You run harder desperate to leave this place forever and not look back, but your hopes are quashed as you can hear loud clicking and hissing from behind. A glance over your shoulders reveals a devastating threat, hundreds of briar arachnids massing the tunnel determined to catch you. Terror grips your entire body as you feel so overwhelmed by their numbers, but you can still escape safely they are far behind you. When you turn your attention back to the exit of the tunnel and notice a lone soldier briar arachnid ahead, blocking your route to safety. You curse your unfortunate luck, as you stare doom coming from either side of you.

If you possess a bow or crossbow and wish to use it turn to **117.**

If you do not possess this weaponry, but would rather use the ability spirit-fire, turn to **173.**

If you do not possess either of these weapons or special abilities turn to **213.**

42

You run as fast as your legs can carry you, but it is not long before you can hear the growling and shouting of the trolls in the distance. You decide to hide behind a tree in hopes that they are unable to track you down. It does not take long though before you can hear them nearby, your skin crawls as they draw ever so nearer to your hiding spot. These are more resilient creatures than you have anticipated.

If you possess the ability of Invisibility and wish to use it turn to **180.**

If you would rather conserve your magic points and remain hidden where you are turn to **242.**

Or if you wish to make a run for it turn to **340.**

43

You calmly reply the name, "Oona." The ferries make a soothing humming noise in surprise that you even know the secret name of the ferry queen. "You must come with us to the enchanted pond." The ferries chant and whisper as they begin to pull you along with them. "Enchanted pond?" You ask full of curiosity. "That is where are home is, and our queen." The ferries respond simultaneously in perfect harmony as if it is one voice that speaks. You obediently follow the ferries through the remainder of the briar patches that litter this area of the forest. Realizing that you truly lost sense of time while you were traveling through the briar arachnid nest, when it should be nightfall you notice that it is almost middle of the next day. You shake your head when you realize how much time you had actually spent in that dark humid nightmare of a place.

You soon arrive in the most beautiful place that you have ever seen; the forest opens into a vibrant large still pure pond. There is sparkling dew that covers the ground the trees, and the air is so fresh and crisp all tension in your entire body is alleviated. The pond is covered in lily pad like housing structures that are stacked one another that these small beings live in, and the powder they secret as they flutter and fly illuminates the entire area brightly. "Welcome outsider, to the Enchanted Pond." Your jaw is agape in disbelief that such perfect tranquility can possible exist here in this treacherous forest. "Wait here tall one." The ferries command as they fly to the other side of the pond, you notice a small grotto there. The twinkling lights of the ferries are flickering inside the cave like wonder in the distance. Suddenly what you gaze upon next leaves you speechless.

Turn to **269.**

44

Using **2** magic points you call upon the elemental plane for aid, you hope they answer your plea. You begin to notice the wind picking up in speed and dropping in temperature, and you witness a gale unlike any other as a cyclone appears on the other side of the burning house. The small tornado grows in size as it pounds the flames into disappearing smoke trails, but you hope the aid of the elementals does more good then harm because your father is inside still alive. As soon as the flames are fanned out enough you enter the structure, and find your father on the ground in the kitchen lying on his back. You kneel beside him and desperately try to heal him and mend his tattered and torn body but he shakes his soot covered face and coughs hoarsely. "It is too late for me my son…, you must find the guild mage.., hurry my son!" Your father whispers with his last breath before his body slackens with the cold embrace of death. You shed your tears for your mother and father, but you must honor your father's last request and find the village guild mage.

Turn to **325.**

45

With the expense of **2** magic points you focus on the glimpse of the future that soon floods your mind, it is more intense than you had expected it to be. Apparently you have entered some kind of a natural network of tunnels; in fact it is a maze. Your insight also informs you there are many dangers that lurk inside this labyrinth, although the destination of where the end of this maze is located is not clear you know that you must find it if you are to reach Allendrah. You can also feel the danger and dark enchantments that shroud you; a cold chill runs down your spine as you try to determine which tunnel to take.

If you possess the guardian ring turn to **109**.
If you wish to take the left tunnel turn to **123**.
If you would rather take the right tunnel, turn to **161**.
If you choose the straight tunnel, turn to **205**.

46

You quickly in one fluid movement have an arrow readied and pointed at the creatures eye, not letting the sounds of the spider horde behind you distract you from your target you release the bolt. Roll the chance dice.

If you rolled 0-4, turn to **103**.
If you rolled 5 or higher turn to **162**.

47

Forcing your nerves to there very limit you fight off the strange effects of the gas cloud that has now engulfed you completely. Your muscles tighten, and your eye lids feel very heavy. Overwhelming grogginess numbs your mind and senses, but you force your will to press onward. The trek to the end of the mushroom field seems endless, but you are determined not to fail and let a gas cloud claim your life. Fatigued and about to drop to your knees you realize that you only have inches to cross before arriving to safety. Your legs feel so heavy, but you use every last bit of strength to cross the threshold to safety. Your exertion has cost you **2** magic points. You take a few minutes to rest and shake off the effects of the gas before continuing on the trail.

Turn to **348.**

48

You barely manage to avoid the shot that was aimed at your heart; the bandit leader appears to be surprised by your reflexes. You have your weapon ready as the bandit leader discards his longbow and draws two black sinister daggers from his belt, "You think you stand a chance against me boy!" Taunts the large man as he paces around you in a combat stance. The bandit leader moves with demonic speed and rushes right at you with a series of slashes with his evil looking weapons, forced into backing up more and more from his deadly attacks you are soon pinned against a tree. "Just give me the stone boy." The bandit leader demands. "Never!" You shout as you manage an offensive attack and force yourself from the tree and attack with your weapon. "Very well boy.., I will enjoy gutting you." If you have fought this bandit leader before you may add **2** to your attack, otherwise deduct **3** from your attack rating.

Falco Drifkan Bandit Leader (Dual wielding demon claw daggers)

Attack. 30   **Health points. 28**
Armor class. 4   **Magic points. 0**

Hit: 1d6 +4 Poison damage.

(Every time that Falco has a successful hit, you must roll the chance to determine if you are poisoned. If you roll under a 4 you are poisoned and take an extra **1d4** poison damage every round until you either use an antidote, or curing to cure the condition.)

If you survive the combat turn to **92.**

49

The strange spider creature moves with blinding speed, and will manage to close the ground between the two of you within the blink of an eye. Your reflexes are just as quick and before you even realize it you have an arrow ready to fire. You must roll the chance dice.

If you rolled 0-3, turn to **91**.
If you rolled 4 or higher turn to **234.**

50

You force your steed to turn down the west path to Balsat, you are not entirely sure if you are heading in the right direction. The only concern on your mind right now is getting away from the bandits that are getting closer. A bandit rider suddenly appears on your left side; with his sword drawn he strikes at your horse. There is a long gash along the thigh of your ride, the horse squeals in pain. You begin to lose control of your steed, and another bandit appears on your right side. You have your weapon ready, and manage to defend yourself from a strike towards your midsection. You must fight these men separately but each for only one round each.

Bandit rider [left side]

Attack. 14   Health points. 16
Armor class. 2   Magic points. 0

Hit: 1d6 +1

Bandit rider [right side]

Attack. 14   Health points. 15
Armor class. 2   Magic points. 0

Hit: 1d6 +1

If your health point total has fallen to **10** or below turn to **126.**

If your health point total is above **10**, turn to **284.**

51

Instinctively you remove the spirit stone from your backpack; its milky white warm glow soothes your entire body. You can feel its divinely good power surging through everything around you; the stone does not deter the bandit leader from his assault. You do however sense and have a better understanding of how he is unable to die by normal means; you can see a shadowy aura around him that is connected to another plane of existence. When the bandit leader notices that the stones powers have been re-awakened he pauses and hisses at the light around you and the stone. "You have to have more than a rock to stop me, prepare to die boy!" Shouts Falco as he resumes his attack. (You must combine your total Health point value with your magic points to combat the evil presence that empowers the bandit leader and roll the chance dice.)

If the score you get is **10** or above turn to **154.**
If the score you get is below **10** turn to **254.**

52

With the cost of **2** magic points you chant in a whisper across this dimension and to the elemental plain for aid, and it does not take long for your call to be heard. The large tree folk cautiously observes as the ground next to it suddenly begins to crack and split, you also marvel in the display of your control over the known elements. Two large stony brown and gray hands reach from the cracks and a clay golem slowly climbs from its hole, the tree folk does not appear to be too impressed. The elementals from the ground are not as intelligent as water, fire, or air elemental would be but they are the easiest to manage. The golem's cold sunken eyes stare at you and the tree folk, "what does wizard want?" Its hoarse voice asks. You and the tree folk exchange glances before you answer the golem, "Dig. Dig a big hole." You command. It nods and in just moments it uses its oversized limbs to create a large hole, after it has finished it crumbles into a lump of clay.

"Indeed you have the knowledge and skill of a Riven mage, I am called Oak Root, the guardian of the Azart Forest. Long have my kin populated the trees of this forest, but still the forest shrinks and continues to die?" Booms the tree folk's loud voice in frustration. You lower your head in sorrow, "I am sorry that man no longer respects the forest, and its beings."

Oak Root smiles at you warmly, "The elves of Allendrah have remained hidden and unseen in their sacred garden for many centuries. Care not do they for the well being of the forest, I have begged for them to intervene but they never leave the garden to help the forest. I will help as best I can …?" "Sabin!" You say as you interrupt the giant. "Sabin… I will help you, but you must accompany me to our domain." Beckons Oak Root. "Our Domain?" You ask full of confusion. Oak Root opens his branch like arms wide and it is then that you notice the other tree folk creatures all around you. They all vary in appearance no two of these massive giants look alike. You count at least five others walking closer towards you and Oak Root.

"They have come to see the last of the Riven clan." States Oak Root as he greets his fellow kin. The first of these monsters to look you up and down is just a hair smaller and thinner than Oak Root. "I am Nettle Branch." It says in a softer whispering like voice. "I am called Leaf Brow." Says the second in deep grunt. Leaf Brow is covered in thick large four pointed green leaves, and has only one glowing green eye. "I am Sage Trunk." Says the second largest of these beings. Sage Trunk has a much thicker base and a lighter coloration than the others and speaks with a hoarse echoing tone. You can feel so much magic emanating from these ancient beings; it is enough to make you feel like a tiny insect. "Well descendant of the Riven clan, will you come with us to the sacred grove?" Oakroot asks.

If you wish to accompany the tree folk to the sacred grove turn to **264.**

If you would rather politely decline their offer and continue your mission, turn to **163.**

53

After Falco dies, you look over his corpse and find the following items that you may make use of.

20 copper
Studded leather vest

Leather gloves
Leather boots
Longbow- Attack. 10 (Damage: 1d8 +2)
<u>Twin Demon claw daggers (If taken must take both)</u>
Attack. 6 (for each)
Damage: 1d4 +1 Poison damage. (Each)

Every successful hit roll the chance dice, any time the number is below 4 the enemy is poisoned and takes extra 1d 4 damage every round of combat.

After you have taken any of the following items and have finished adjusting your character sheet you may continue by turning to **350.**

54

You do not find anything of importance on the first couple of skeletons on the ground, but something shiny is one of the skeletons fingers on the ground next to the roaring fire in the center of the chamber. A closer look reveals a single copper key, it is old faded and covered in dust. You take the light weight key your hand, (mark this as a special item.) You wish you knew what this key unlocked? You stare around the room until you notice a keyhole on the wall farthest from the staircase; you closely examine the keyhole and realize that the copper key would fit perfectly and that it is in fact the key that is used for that lock.

If you wish to use the key on this keyhole turn to **144.**
If you would rather not risk setting off another trap and wish to leave the danger of the crypt, turn to **121.**

55

The second rider charges into the fray and swings his sword at you, blocking the blow with your weapon the loud clang of steel against steel echoes loudly. You cannot evade the combat and must them both as one enemy. (Deduct 2 from your attack rating, due to your attackers being on horseback.)

Bandit horsemen

Attack. 25   Health points. 30
Armor class.   4Magic points. 0

Hit: 2d6 +2

If you survive the combat turn to **72**.

56

You stand in combat as the troll duo rapidly closes in on you, this combat cannot be avoided you must these two as one enemy.

Trolls

Attack. 26   Health points. 34
Armor class. 2   Magic points. 0

Hit: 1d10 +3

After both of the large lumbering trolls fall to the ground dead, you only find two copper coins and the club that one

carried. (If you want to keep the club it has the same item benefits that # 3 mace has on the weapons list for you to refer to.) You do not hesitate to flee the troll encampment.

Turn to **3.**

57

The tunnel leading downward makes your skin crawl, there is a foul musky odor in the air, the ground is covered in sticky thick mud with rotted forest debris in it. It is so dark that if you have not already lit a torch you must do so, (If you do not possess a torch you must use **1** magic point to create a light source.) It is humid and uncomfortable; you wipe sweat as it pours down your face. After a mile or so of trekking this place you walk into a large chamber with dozens of large white back pack sized pulsating sac's that are stuck to the walls. You cannot help but be slightly curious by the strange spectacle before you.

Turn to **315.**

58

You push open the poorly assembled door to the tavern, the smell of tobacco smoke and dust hit your senses violently. You take slow breaths as you walk over towards the counter where the barkeep stands starring you up and down suspiciously. "What can I get you outlander?" The large pot bellied barkeep hoarsely barks. The man is very tall; broad shouldered, and has a bald head. "Pint of bitter will run you one copper stranger? And the house special is our roast for another copper." You realize that you are quite hungry, if you wish to have a meal provided for you and the pint of bitter it will cost you two copper. Otherwise you must eat a meal from your backpack or loose **3** health points. A glance of your surroundings reveals only four other people inside the tavern, three of which sit at a table in a private conversation. The fourth man is sitting alone with his head in his hands.

If you wish to question the lone stranger about the Azart Forest, turn to **116**.

Or if you would rather question the three other men at the table in a private conversation, turn to **186.**

If you would prefer to obtain information by leaving the tavern and entering the Herbalist shop, turn to **102.**

Or if you decide to obtain information at the smithy turn to **208.**

59

The tiny sprites manage to conjure up a variety of different deliciousness for you to devour, fruits, berries, mushrooms, and tubers. You feast upon the smorgasbord of food until you have had your fill, the fae observe as you finish the platter of food quickly. "Now rest young Sabin, there will be a full day ahead of with the dawn. For the next midday we arrive to Allendrah." Just the thought of your long mission being completed relaxes you enough to fall into a deep slumber. As you slumber though, your dreams are haunted by frightening visage of events that cannot possibly be real?

In your nightmare you see a wave of darkness that stretches over everything; you also see a blood red moon high in the sky. Fiery molten rocks crash down from the heavens and lay waste to many of the civilizations that cover Lamara. Strange evil creatures pour from a black abyss and wash over the land like a plague; you see despair and death everywhere. Worst of all you see a fearsome figure behind it all, a woman the most sinister looking woman that you have ever seen looking into you deeply. "You will fail." She hisses in a snake like tone that sends chills down your spine. The woman has attractive features but has evil red eyes, long flowing red hair, long devilish horns, pointed ears, large tattered bat like wings, cloven hoofed feet, and long sharp black nails. "This world belongs to me!" She adds. You awake screaming and covered in sticky cold sweat.

Turn to **267.**

60

Before too long you notice that the sun has set, and you can make out the shape of the full moon in the sky. Your first night in the Azart Forest has you completely nervous and extremely paranoid. In the daylight the forest is scary enough, but alone in the black darkness of this forest you cannot help but be full of terror. (If you possess a torch you must use for a light source. If not you must use **1** magic point to cast a small orb of light so that you can see through the dark.) Red eyes dot your surroundings, and the sounds of the wildlife grow even louder. As you slowly follow the barely visible trail the howling wind blows across the back of your neck sending a cold chill down your spine. The loud unsettling hoot of a owl startles you as you try to keep your eyes on the trail. Soon you can feel fatigue taking its effect on your mind; you decide to make a small campsite along the trial next to a fallen hallowed out tree trunk. (You must eat a meal or lose **4** health points.) You start a small fire in hopes to repel any curious wildlife in the area as you prepare to rest for the evening.

Turn to **166.**

61

You continue through the winding passage, looking over your shoulder as if expecting an ambush from these terrifying spider that thrive all over the place here. You carefully peek around every corner you arrive at until the tunnel forks into two different directions, one tunnel leads upward, and the other leads downward.

If you wish to take the tunnel leading upward turn to **41.**

If you would rather go downward turn to **211.**

62

After closely studying the message of the riddle you notice a dark almost black oak like tree just to your left, and you also notice that the leaves are split to make a six edge leaf.

The next detail that catches your attention is more black trees growing that grow in a single direction, making sense of the correlation between this and the riddle that you have just red you follow the direction that the trees are growing in until you do not see another black tree. You stop and wonder if you really are heading in the right direction, until a howling gentle breeze blows past you and you notice a owl statue beside a large tree. You notice that is very life like but one of the eyes that is carved into the granite has a small piece of red ruby in it, but the other eye is just an empty socket. Another peculiar detail that you immediately notice is that the socket that is carved into the stone is shaped a arrow pointing in the direction that you must head. At last the riddle makes complete sense to you.

If you wish to try and pry the ruby free from the owl statue turn to **100.**

If you would rather just walk in the direction laid out before you turn to **188.**

63

After your enemies are slain, you immediately flee the scene in case more decide to appear and attack. The tunnel continues to turn and slope upward and downward sporadically, you cautiously peek around every corner to make sure there are no more lurking threats awaiting you on the other side. Before too long though the tunnel splits into two different directions, one direction is upward, and the other is downward.

If you wish to go upward turn to **41.**

If you choose to go downward turn to **211.**

64

Your quick reactions allow you to barely leap out of range of the burning wood from smashing you, but you notice the entire roof is collapsing around you. Desperately you try to flee the danger, but you feel a large chunk of burnt wood strike you in the back and you immediately fall to the ground unconscious. Unable to move to safety the smoke claims your life before the fire and collapsing roof does.

Your life and quest end here.

65

The large soldier briar arachnid topples over dead, and you have just enough time to continue your escape from this place and the horde of spiders that is closing in on you. The light from the exit of the tunnel continues to motivate you to escape to safety, but you're so exhausted from fighting and running. It seems like you are moving in slow motion as you approach the exit, the second you are out of the tunnel and back in the expanse of the Azart Forest you feel as if a great weight has lifted itself from your shoulders. You take a deep breath of fresh air, and fight the burn from your exhausted muscles. You are not out of harms way just yet.

Turn to **187.**

66

You are beginning to panic, as the bandits close in. The two horsemen appear at both sides of you and have they're weapons drawn for an attack. You manage to defend blow for blow, but you must wound them enough to manage an escape. (You must fight the horsemen as one enemy for two rounds of combat.)

2 Bandit horsemen

Attack. 25   **Health points. 30**
Armor class. 4   **Magic points. 0**

Hit: 2d6 +2

After several intense exchanges of attacks, one rider loses balance of his steed and falls backwards. The other is wounded enough to fall behind, Falco the leader pushes passed his henchmen and quickly closes the gap between his men. His hateful eyes burn into you, "prepare for a real fight boy." Taunts the bandit leader as he draws his weapon and begins to attack you. After what seems a long exchange of attacks between you and the leader of the bandits, you manage strike him upside the head and knock him from his mount. The furious bandit leader rolls on the ground shouting at you, and soon disappears from sight. You sigh that you have managed to escape your enemies.

Turn to **174.**

67

The left tunnel leads you up and then downward, soon you are ankle deep in pools of stagnant water. The smell of this tunnel does not settle well with your stomach, it is the foul stench of rotten vegetation and death. You force yourself onward, keeping a close eye on the path ahead and behind your shoulders. After several more minutes a new threat stops you in your tracks, ahead you notice a large spider walking towards you. But this one is different from the others of its kind, it is jet black, and has oversized forearms. The second its large ink black eye notices you, it clicks loudly and hisses before it charges at you. It is far quicker than the other spiders as well, you cannot evade this fight.

Soldier Briar Arachnid

Attack. 14   **Health points. 18**

Armor class. 1   **Magic points. 0**

Hit: 1d6 +3

(Remember that these creatures are weak to fire, incendiary potions and spirit-fire damage is doubled.)

If you survive the combat turn to **171.**

68

You explain who you are, and why you in this beings domain. The large tree patiently listens, but with a skeptical expression on its large face. After you have told your story the large tree huffs loudly at you, and points its long solid branch for a arm at you. "I do not believe thou, the Riven mages have all died out you are a deceiver. Thou shall not pass!" The grumbling of the massive tree being shakes the very forest floor. You plead your desperation to find Allendrah and seek guidance from the elves, but the giant lumbering hulk waves his branch dismissively at you. "Away with you!" It roars, as it continues to block you from proceeding. You must find a way to prove your story if you are to continue your quest.

If you wish to show the being the spirit stone, in hopes of proving who you are turn to **125.**

Or if you would prefer to use one of your magical abilities to prove you are a descendant of the Riven mage clan turn to **153.**

If you choose to attack this being that hinders your mission progression, turn to **304.**

69

You nervously reply the name, "Zfendell!" The fae's docile expression soon turns into a sinister expression that you quickly regret seeing. "You are not welcome in our realm intruder." The small creature hisses as the others of its kind swarm around you aggressively, they fly around you so quickly that you become very dizzy. You are unable to make out anything around you, seeing only blurs and feel like you are moving to fast you drop to your knees and clutch your hands to your head protectively. After you shrug off the dizziness, you open your eyes and slowly rise to your shaking feet. The fae are gone, and you are no longer in place that you recognize. You also notice that the spirit stone is no longer in your possession; the little sneaks have taken it somehow from you. You are in a part of this forest that is unfamiliar to you, and you spend the rest of your days going in circles until you starve to death.

You have failed your quest, and your life ends here.

70

Immediately a cold chill runs down your spine as you trek into the mysterious silence of the graveyard, a thin layer of white mist hangs over the ashen ground and the shadows of the old worn and weathered tombstones dancing around in the moonlight. A single black raven with red beady eyes sits on the tallest of these tombstones and stares at you menacingly; you bite your lip and swallow a large lump that appears in your throat. The crow suddenly caws loudly before departed its perch and flies past you keeping its red eyes on you, and a cold breeze blows in your face that smells faintly of dirt and something that you cannot explain? The first tomb stone that you come across draws your attention, you notice that there is no name on this one instead there are strange markings. After you have looked over the tombs that litter the area, you notice there are three tombstones without names? You wonder why there are three with no names, but you wonder if a closer look would reveal the answer?

If you wish to examine the tombstones more closely turn to **196.**
If you would rather ignore the tombstones and explore the crypt just ahead turn to **253.**

Holding the spirit stone tightly in both hands, you concentrate on pushing your body to the limits as the spider horde advances upon you. Suddenly you feel a surge of phenomenal power coursing through your entire body; the spirit stone has just cast a golden aura around you. There is a slight humming noise as you feel your muscles tighten as the magic of all the Riven magi before you take your powers to a new plateau that you have never experienced before. The spider horde is upon you; instinctively you throw your arms up into the air and the first wave of briar arachnids are forced into the sky in pieces. Every movement you make sends waves of psionic energy into your enemies and renders them into shards of what they once were, and every spider that manages to attack you is unable to cause any damage to you. Several try to spit their acidic salvia on you, but it does not burn or even irritate your skin. The green fluids just drip off from you onto the ground. The power of the spirit stone is impressive, and far more dangerous than you had thought. A second onslaught of spider's moves on you, using your weapon and legs you quickly hack the remaining arachnids until every single spider is dead. Taking a moment to rest you bask in the warming soothing glow of the spirit stone, (restore all lost health points and magic points to their original levels.) Just as you prepare to continue your quest something new catches your eyes.

Turn to **241.**

72

You land the killing blows on the bandit horsemen, both corpses crash to the ground the steeds which they were upon go tearing off into the wilderness. A search of the body's turns up a combined total of 6 copper coins, two daggers, two swords, and a in tact leather studded vest. (If worn adds 1 to your armor class value.) You decide to get moving before bandits decide to survey this location, and discover that the two horsemen were overcome by a single villager. You quickly run off for the Lorna grasslands.

Turn to **36**.

73

You enhanced hearing tells you that the clicking noises are coming from just ahead, but from who or what is making the noise is a complete mystery? The clicking grows louder and louder, and now there is a scraping noise. You bite your lip nervously as you try to come up with an idea of how to avoid detection by whatever is rapidly approaching.

If you possess the ability Invisibility and wish to use it turn to **104**.

If you do not possess this ability and would rather turn back the way you came turn to **113**.

If you choose to wait and attack whatever is approaching turn to **164**.

74

With your palm extended, you release a searing jet of hissing flames at the tiny arachnids. They scream and squeal as they are burn to ashes; the use of this ability has cost you **1** magic point. The few remaining young that did not become engulfed by the fire retreat back to the brood chamber, you stop to catch your breath and recover in the humid tunnel. Sweat pours from your forehead, and your clothes are stuck to your skin. After a brief moment of recovery you begin to continue along the tunnel, until a loud clicking noise stops you in your tracks. Suddenly two briar arachnids appear at the head of the tunnel, their large inky cold black eyes lock onto you. They immediately hiss and charge towards you with frightening speed.

If you possess a bow or crossbow and wish to use it turn to **120.**

If you do not possess such weaponry and would rather use the ability Spirit-Fire, turn to **159.**

If you do not possess either weapons, or this ability turn to **201.**

75

At last the hulking living tree monster gives a dying wail before crashing to the forest floor loudly and shaking the ground, it becomes a mass of splintered broken pieces of wood. A closer look at this being reveals that it is very ancient, and perhaps a guardian of this forest. You also notice a large nut on the ground beside it; it is about the size of your palm. It is oval shaped with smooth edges and a light brown complexion. This is a Gava nut, very rare and sacred. These nuts have the power to fully restore ones health and spiritual energies. If you wish to take this nut mark it as a backpack item. (Gava nut: restores all lost health points and magic points.) Without further delay you continue to trek the trail and continue your quest.

Turn to **163.**

76

You quickly turn and flee; the two arachnids are quickly behind your feet. Suddenly you trip and fall on a loose rock on the ground, after you land on the floor in the mud the spiders on upon you. Searing pain shoots at your side when you notice a large cut from a swinging saw like arm. You lose **1d4** health points, and you are quickly on your feet avoiding attacks from the spider duo. You must fight these two creatures to the death, and you cannot evade the combat.

2 Soldier Briar Arachnids

Attack. 26   **Health points. 30**
Armor class. 2   **Magic points. 0**

Hit: 1d12 +3

(Remember these creatures are weak to fire, incendiary potions and spirit-fire damage is doubled.)
If you survive the combat turn to **63.**

77

At the cost of **4** magic points you call onto the spirit world,
your chant is quickly heard and you can feel a dark presence
surround you. Black infinite shadows appear and swirl and

dance all around you, a cold chill runs down your spine as you realize that you have chosen incorrectly. Suddenly the two sarcophagus begin to shake and move. "You have failed!" Echoes a loud deathly low toned voice as you watch the covers of the sarcophagus open and the stone door behind you slams shut. To your horror, the corpses inside the tombs begin to move and rise from their eternal rest. This was a test, one to separate good from evil. This ancient trap is unstoppable, and you must overcome it. The two mostly decayed bodies bear the tunics of your ancestors but the bodies are possessed by evil forces from your own spell, and now the undead have come to collect your soul. The zombies slowly advance towards you hungry for brains; with limbs stretched out they reach for you. You must fight these undead imposters.

Zombies [Undead]

Attack. 15   **Health points. 30**
Armor class. 2   **Magic points. 0**

Hit: 1d8 +1

After you land the final strike on the two undead beings the corpses collapse to the dirty dusty floor of the crypt and then disintegrate into a pile of dust and bones. Next the crypt door begins to grind and move open again; you wipe a single bead of sweat from your brow and sigh.

If you wish to use the ability Spirit-Fire, turn to **228.**

If you choose to use Elementalism turn to **137.**

If you do not possess either of these abilities you must leave the crypt by turning to **121.**

78

You raise your shield and prepare for the arrow bolt, you hear the release of the bowstring and the bandit leader watches as your shield rises for the incoming missile. The arrow strikes the shield with a loud thump, and the force of the bolt sends you backwards on your backside. Falco curses your move, and hands his bow to one of his many men that now begin to surround the area. You quickly get back on your feet and begin to run again, but when you glance over your shoulder you notice the bandit leader hopping onto a saddle of a black stallion. You can hear the shouts of other horsemen in the distance; you need to quickly find a way to escape you will not be able to outrun them without a horse yourself. As you near the end of the town you notice a stable ahead and several horses are tied to a fence post, you quickly untie one of them and hop on the back of one without a saddle. Not sure of how to correctly direct a hose you grab the reins and shout forward, but the horse does nothing. Your heart sinks in a wave of panic as the bandits and their leader close in; you shout and kick the horse's sides with your heel in hopes of getting it to move. Then you pull the pull the reins one more time and without warning the horse tears off, you almost fall of your ride as it moves with impressive speed.

Turn to **155.**

79

You are immediately locked into combat with no ordinary briar arachnid; this is a soldier, a fighter for its hive. The creature slashes at you with its oversized saw like forearms, you jump back surprised by its lightning quick speed. You cannot evade this fight; you must kill this creature if you are to survive.

Soldier Briar Arachnid

Attack. 14   **Health points. 18**
Armor class. 1   **Magic points. 0**

Hit: 1d6 +3

(These creatures are weak to fire, incendiary potions and spirit-fire damage is doubled.)

If you win the combat turn to **142.**

80

Without realizing it at first, the moment you think about how you are going to find Allendrah without the convenience of a trail the branches of all the nearby trees begin to creak and move. You watch as every branch points to the west, you are relieved that you have this special magical ring. You would not be able to accurately navigate this immense forest without it. You whisper a thanks to Oak Root for his generous gift.

If you wish to head west as indicated by the guardian ring turn to **217.**

If you do not trust the ring and would rather use the ability Fore- Sight to determine the direction you should take to reach Allendrah turn to **110.**

Or if you do not possess the ability of fore-sight and would rather use enhanced senses turn to **135.**

If you do not possess either of these abilities and do not trust the guardian ring, turn to **236**.

81

You gather all of your equipment, and Oona returns the spirit stone to your charge. "You must carry this to the elves; your fate is our fate Sabin." You nod and place the stone back inside your backpack, (Remember to record this item in a slot on your character sheet.) There is a cast of several pixies that surround you and Oona, her royal escort you assume. "When we set foot out of the enchanted pond we are no longer protected by its magic, we will be wide open to the many perils of the forest." States Oona with concern on her smooth silken face. You follow the sprites and they're leader out of the protective magic of the enchanted pond, the emptiness and darkness of the Azart Forest surround you now. Sunlight attempts to poke out of the tree line from above, but the oppressive dark branches from the hollow trees blot out as much of it as possible. "There is an evil force here!" Oona whispers and pauses starring around the forest as if she can something that no one could. "The forest never used to be like this!" Adds the ferry queen as she shivers from the ominous surroundings. You watch as her large crimson wings allow her to hover over the forest floor at a pace that you are beginning to have trouble keeping up with. Hours pass slowly as you trudge onward; you get the feeling that you are being watched again. A constant look over your shoulder to make sure that there are no monsters getting ready to spring out of the shadows reassures your nerves slightly. The fae stop abruptly when you hear a twig snap from the distance.

If you possess the ability enhanced senses and wish to use them turn to **152.**

If you do not possess this ability or would rather use Fore-Sight, turn to **179.**

If you do not possess either of these abilities roll the chance dice.

If you rolled 0-3, turn to **197.**

If you rolled a 4 or higher turn to **243.**

82

The strange half plant half spider monster swings its slashing arm towards you, ducking the attack you jump back and attempt to attack it with your weapon. The spider's reflexes are far quicker than you predicted and it completely avoids your attack and leaps to the ceiling of the tunnel making high pitched clicking noises. You prepare yourself as it launches its second attack.

Briar Arachnid

Attack. 10   **Health points. 13**
Armor class. 1   **Magic points. 0**

Hit: 1d4 +3

(This creature has a weakness to fire, incendiary potions and spirit-fire damage is doubled.)

You may evade the combat after the first round of combat by turning to **157.**

If you survive turn to **195.**

83

With a swift kick to the bandit's groin you manage to buy enough time to turn and run, but he recovers from the blow quickly and is in pursuit. The bandit shouts for help from his fellow men, and two more bandits appear for the chase. You need to gain enough ground to hide and elude the enemy, roll the chance dice.

If you rolled 0-4, turn to **190**.
Of if you rolled 5 or higher turn to **310.**

84

You softly answer the question by uttering the name, "Alleriah." The fae look on you with disappointment and suspicion, as you realize that you have not replied with the correct name. Without warning the magical pixie dust that is covering you begins to sting painfully, you cry out pain as you attempt to flee from the tiny sprites. However the dust has another debilitating effect, as you realize that you are unable to move. Your last moments are spent trying to scream in pain as the dust melts you into a pool of dead matter.

Your life and quest end here.

85

Using extreme caution, you slowly creep in the direction that the smell is coming from. Hiding behind a large thorn bush you hear the crackling and snapping of a roaring campfire, just beyond the bush you notice a large skinned animal hanging from a thick rope tied to pole next to the fire. The smell makes your mouth water, and your stomach roar. You have never smelled meat cooking like this, you cannot resist wanting some for yourself. You do not see anyone near the campfire, which strikes you as odd because someone or something had to have been preparing this meal. You

pause for a moment in hopes of the one responsible for this campsite returning, but after the pause you see no one.

If you wish to attempt to take some of the cooking meat, turn to **132**.

If you would rather continue your quest, turn to **318.**

If you possess the ability of Fore-sight and wish to use it turn to **148.**

86

After almost an hour of trekking a winding humid damp tunnel, you soon arrive at a fork in the tunnels. There is a tunnel going upward and one going downward.

If you wish to take the tunnel going upward, turn to **202**.

If you choose the tunnel leading downward turn to **274.**

87

You lash out violently at the mushrooms as they continue to spew orange gas from their large caps, but as the poison touches your skin you can feel your muscles tightening and movement soon becomes very difficult. The more orange gas you inhale the more fatigued you become, before you know it you on your knees unable to move. You fall face first into the ground paralyzed and in a deep sleep in which you will never awaken.

Your have fallen victim to one of the many perils of the Azart Forest, your life and quest end here!

88

You attempt to free yourself by using you weapon, but the troll is already on you. You dodge the first strike it tries to land on you with its makeshift club by swing away from its range; however the second strike you are unable to avoid. The wooden club hits you in the side of the head, your ears ring and your head is pounding. Your skull is cracked and you fight to stay conscious but due to your stunned delay you are struck again in the torso and you are unable to even gasp in agony. You immediately feel all of your strength sapped from your body, and the trolls third and most powerful strike is enough to instantly kill you.

Your life and quest end here.

89

You aim for Falco's head and fire your weapon, and watch as the bolt flies towards its target. You however were not expecting the bandit leader to dodge the attack at the last second as he sidesteps the shot and your arrow flies into the ground. You must act quickly; Falco will be upon you in seconds.

If you wish to attempt another shot turn to **183.**

If you would prefer to use the power of the spirit stone to stop your enemy, turn to **51**.

90

You very slowly creak open the large wooden door, and cautiously enter the small one room hut. You see the elder standing in the corner of the hut with his back to you; he is wearing his traditional blue robe with a very small golden trim along the sleeves, and his wooden cap. He short and very old, "Sabin. I have been waiting for you." The elder's creaky voice echoes throughout the entire hut. He turns slowly his white azure eyes pierce into your very soul and his long beak like nose twitches slightly at the sight of you. "We are under attack! What do we do?" You plead as you approach the wise village elder. The man smiles at you warmly, "I am afraid there are far too many of them young one. There is nothing we can do." The icy words of the elder sting you harshly, "Surely out magic can save us all!" You plead as your shake the old man by his scrawny shoulders.

The elder shakes his head, and lowers his sorrowful eyes to the ground. "They are after the one thing that we cannot allow them to have Sabin." The guild mage points to a small chest. You can only guess that the sacred spirit stone is inside, "What do we do then?" You ask. The elder walks over to the small chest and slowly opens it, inside is the most sacred relic of all Lamara. The spirit stone is about the size of your palm, you can feel its warm aura of milky white power surging through everything. "We cannot let these evil men obtain this artifact; it is our duty to make sure that will never happen!" The guild mage states sternly starring into your eyes.

You nod, and pace around the center room waiting for the elder to come up with a plan. "The stone must make its way home to Allendrah!" Your jaw drops with shock, you have heard that name before but you were never really sure if such a place ever existed. Allendrah is the home of the true Lamaran Guardians, the elves. Creators and true masters of magic, they created the spirit stone to allow man to use magic. The stone was given to the Riven clan, the first humans to wander Lamara under elven guidance. The pact was that as long as man could keep balance and the stone safe man was worthy of the benefits of magic.

Allendrah is the secret city of the elves hidden deep within the dangerous Azart forest. "How are we supposed to get the stone back to Allendrah?" You ask. The guild mage's eyes twinkle slightly as he stares upon with the answer. "You have just answered your own question my young apprentice." You shake your head in protest at such a crazed notion. "I am not ready for such responsibility, I require more training." The guild mage shakes his head and waves his free hand at you, "nonsense! You have learned all that I can teach you. Now you must put what you have learned to the test Sabin, you must take the stone to Allendrah. It will be safe back in the elves hands, if you do this then you will have proved yourself worthy of being my successor." You swallow a very large lump in your throat, still in shock by everything that is happening you drop to your knees and take a very long deep breath. "Quickly we do not have much time Sabin…My fore-sight has revealed that they will be here very soon." You stand shaking in your boots as you accept this perilous quest.

Turn to **280.**

91

You fire your arrow at the spider creature, but quicker than your eyes can follow it avoids the attack completely and leaps at you. You sidestep from the creatures slashing serrated edged fore arms, and attempt to attack the creatures abdomen. Your attack is quick, but the spider leaps onto the ceiling of the tunnel making loud clicking noises. Its large eye is starring intently at you as its mouth and abdomen begin to retract, and you can tell that is going to expel something from its mouth. The half plant half spider creature spews òut a single stream of green fluid, you jump barely out of the path of the spit. You immediately feel a burning sensation on your arm, and you notice that a couple of drops of the strange fluid are burning your clothes and skin. The creature can secret some kind of acid, you take **1d4** damage. You must be wary of this creatures arms as well as its acid. You stand on guard as the creature attacks you from the ceiling.

Briar Arachnid

Attack. 10   **Health points. 13**
Armor class. 1   **Magic points. 0**

Hit: 1d4 +3

(This strange creature as a strong aversion towards fire, incendiary potions and spirit-fire damage is doubled.)

If you survive the combat turn to **195.**

92

You land the killing strike that sends the bandit leader to his knees; your tightened muscles relax as you sigh with relief. But to your horror the bandit leader laughs evilly, "Do you really think that it would be that easy to defeat me boy?" You look on in shock as Falco rises to his feet, his fatal wounds do not seem to bring death to this warrior. "But how?" You ask completely confused by how this man is still standing. "I am no ordinary man; I serve a god and higher purpose. Your conventional weapons will not slay me boy! Now I will destroy you, and have the stone." Hisses Falco as he doubles his efforts in another attack and comes charging at you with inhuman speed. You must act quickly if you are to beat this seemingly invincible foe.

If you wish to stand your ground and fight this man, turn to **149**.

Or if you would rather use the special ability fore-sight to discover the means of his unnatural powers turn to **177**

If you do not possess this power and would rather use the ability spirit-fire, turn to **252.**

If you do not have either of these abilities and would rather use a bow/or crossbow to slow him down turn to **261.**

Or if you feel the power of the spirit stone can stop this madman turn to **51.**

93

The current only gets stronger as it pulls deeper and deeper into the water, your strength is quickly being sapped from you as you try to remain in control. You are suddenly pulled under the water and pushed against a large rock, your lungs ache for air as you struggle to free yourself from this underwater prison. You must roll the chance dice.

If you rolled 0-4, turn to **290**.
If you rolled 5 or higher turn to **141.**

94

Amplifying your senses to their maximum you carefully read the entire area around you, and you have an immediate sense of dread overwhelm you. This is the most intense feeling that your enhanced senses have ever felt, you can smell, taste, and sense intense evil and mysterious magic all around you. You get the most sinister feeling in the tunnel directly ahead of you; the sensation is not as evil around the other two.

If you wish to take the tunnel leading left turn to **123**.
If you choose the tunnel leading right instead turn to **161.**
If you prefer the danger of the tunnel straight ahead turn to **205.**

95

You run for the door, and the bandits immediately spring into action to intercept you. "Seize him!" Shouts Falco as his cold stare burns into your soul. Two bandits are now blocking your path and you must fight your way out. (This combat will only last one round.)

Bandits

Attack. 25   **Health points. 28**
Armor class. 3   **Magic points. 0**

Hit: 2d6+2

After one round of combat you manage to escape the tavern, but they are hot on your heels with the leader right behind them.

Turn to **6.**

96

Your second shot hit's the spider and kills it instantly; you sigh with relief and put your weapon away. You continue along the passage, it winds and turns endlessly. You cautiously peek around every corner to make sure there are no hidden threats around the corner, and you keep glancing over your shoulder to make sure that nothing is attempting to creep up on you. Soon the tunnel splits into two different directions, one leading upward and the other direction going downward.

If you wish to go upward turn to **41.**
If you would prefer to go downward turn to **211.**

97

You turn and run as fast you can from these beasts, they immediately pursue you. You find it difficult to run fast enough to elude them without the smooth terrain of a trail, you constantly have to hop over obstructions in your path and sidestep passed the trees that are all over. You can hear the loud breathing of these large feral animals as they bite at your heels, you will not be able to outrun them you must fight these animals one at a time to the death.

Wolf 1

Attack. 10   Health points. 14
Armor class. 1   Magic points. 0

Hit: 1d6 +1

Wolf 2

Attack. 11   Health points. 12
Armor class. 1   Magic points. 0

Hit: 1d6

Wolf 3

Attack. 9   Health points. 11
Armor class. 1   Magic points. 0

Hit: 1d6

Wolf 4

Attack. 10   Health points. 12

Armor class. 1   **Magic points. 0**

Hit: 1d6 +1

If your health point total has fallen below **10** turn to **168.**

If your health point total is above **10** Turn to **225.**

98

Your arrow just misses its target; Falco laughs at your skill with the weapon and does not relent from his attack. "You are going to have to do better than that!" He shouts as he closes in.

If you wish to fire another shot at the bandit leader in hopes of putting him down turn to **183.**

Or if you choose to use the spirit stone turn to **51.**

99

You quickly turn your steed around and head straight at the bandits; they seem surprised by your sudden change of course. Falco orders his men to stand against you, by the time you get within range they are on the attack. (You must fight for one round of combat.)

Bandit horsemen

Attack. 25   **Health points. 30**
Armor class. 4   **Magic points. 0**

Hit: 2d6 +2

You succeed in buying enough time to fend off the bandit attack and push passed the horsemen before Falco can arrive. You charge full speed ahead on the path, and Falco is prepared to meet you head on, his powerful steed with nostrils flaring also charges right for you. You bite your lip nervously though when you are within range of Falco's weapon, with a powerful swing his sword fly's towards you. With quick reflexes you dodge the blow, but the sharp weapon grazes your arm dealing **1d6** damage to you. When the bandit leader notices that he has missed he curses loudly. Soon you find the sign that you passed earlier.

Turn to **293.**

100

Using your weapon you try to pry the single small round ruby out of the socket in which it was inserted in, but the task even more difficult than you thought it would be. It is as if some unseen magical force is binding this gem to the stone of the statue, but after you are about to give up the small gem falls to the ground. You pick it up and examine it closely to make sure it is a real ruby, it has been cut from a much bigger ruby but it is real. (You may keep the small ruby as a backpack item. Ruby's sell for **20** copper or more depending on perfection of the cut.) After you pocket your small treasure you prepare to walk in the direction that the arrow was pointing towards, but you notice that the visual of the terrain ahead begin to shift and change as if the forest is moving.

If you possess the ability of Fore-sight and wish to use it turn to **219.**

If you do not possess this ability and wish to return the ruby from where it came from turn to **260.**

Or if wish to keep the gem and head in the direction that the arrow was pointing turn to **312.**

101

This evil force is overcoming the power of the spirit stone, you need to channel more energy into the stone to fight this powerful darkness and banish it back to where it came from. Falco laughs, "Nothing can stop the power of the matron foolish boy!" You grind your teeth together as you try to will more strength into the stone, but the evil is far to powerful for you to combat and you are completely drained of energy and now defenseless. Falco notices your weakness and takes advantage of the situation; you are unable to stop him and the demon power that resides within in him.

You are slain by an evil force, your life and quest end here.

102

You enter the herbalist ship, the small one room hovel smells faintly of sage and candles. The walls have tall shelves that are filled with various herbs, potions, and remedies. "Welcome to Anna's remedies and herbs shop." An old woman's voice pipes greeting you as you cautiously enter the shop. An old short round woman appears at the front desk with a wide smile on her wrinkled face, she has one eye with a completely white iris, and the other is gray. "Whatever ails you or whatever potion you need I have for sale in my shop." She beckons as she points to the many shelves filled with all kinds of potions and herbs.

Green moss potion -Heals 4 health points. Cost: **2 copper**
Red moss potion -Deals 6 fire damage in combat. Cost: **3 copper**
Antidote -Cures any status ailment. Cost: **2 copper**
Elixir - Restores 4 magic points. Cost: **4 copper**
Empty vial - Must have to mix potions with herbalism. Cost: **1 copper**
(Must have special ability Herbalism to mix listed potions below.)
Spine Root -When mixed into potion with Gamma leaf deals 1d6 damage in combat, and drops enemy attack by 1 point for two rounds. Cost: **2 copper per root.**
Gamma Leaf - Can be mixed with various potions. Drops enemy attack by 1 point for two rounds. Cost: **1copper per leaf.**
Dragon scale -When mixed with Red moss creates dragon fire potion. Deals 1d12 +5 fire damage in combat. Cost: **5 copper per scale.**
Fury Herb -When used in combat adds **3** to attack rating for 2 rounds of combat. When used out of combat adds **2** to the next chance dice roll. Cost: **4 copper per plant.**

After you have finished purchasing any potions, and/or herbs make the proper adjustments to your character sheet. You ask the shop keep about the Azart forest but the lonely woman shrugs her shoulders before leaving the counter.

If you wish to obtain information by entering the tavern, turn to **58**.

Or if you would rather obtain information inside the smithy turn to **208**.

103

You let the bolt loose, it sails true towards it intended target. However the arachnid moves with such speed and agility that it leaps from the arrows path to safety, you curse your luck. You glance back over your shoulder and notice the spider horde, you must keep moving. With great speed you run towards the black spider, you must fight this creature if you are to continue your mission and outrun the spider horde behind you. The large arachnid welcomes your attack.

Soldier Briar Arachnid

Attack. 14   **Health points. 18**
Armor class. 1   **Magic points. 0**

Hit: 1d6 +3

(These creatures are weak to fire, incendiary potions and spirit-fire damage is doubled.)

If you win the combat in three rounds or less turn to **65**.

If you win the combat in three rounds or more turn to **136.**

104

You hurriedly whisper the chant of your spell, and at the cost of **3** magic points you suddenly become completely invisible. You remain motionless as two strange creatures appear in the tunnel next to you; they appear to be large spiders about three feet tall. They are bright green and black, with a single black eye in the center of their heads. Their thorax look similar to the briar plants that make up the tunnel, and they both have two forearms with serrated jagged spikes on them. Their bulbous abdomens pulsate and twitch rapidly as they make strange clicking noises to one another; you assume that is how these strange half plant half spiders communicate with each other. They do not seem aware of your presence, but they refuse to continue traveling the tunnel. The spells effect will not last much longer, you must decide on what do to.

If you wish to move past them and continue down the tunnel turn to **222.**

If you would rather remain still in hopes they do not notice you and move on before the effects of Invisibility ware off turn to **301.**

105

You narrowly escape the effects of the gas cloud, but you can feel the numbness and exhaustion finally subsiding as you catch your breath and regain your strength. You sigh with relief that your abilities came through and you escaped certain death and peril.

Turn to **348.**

106

You continue to remain just from arms length of the bears massive deadly slashing paws, but your entire body aches from extreme exhaustion. Your legs burn like they are covered in flames, and your lungs and heart pound loudly in your chest. The bear roars in frustration from its inability to rend you to pieces, suddenly you notice that your beginning to slow your pace and you are feeling unable to go on.

If you possess the special ability Tolerance and wish to use it turn to **193.**

If you do not possess this ability you must prepare for combat by turning to **232.**

107

As you manage to land the killing blow on the third arachnid, the fourth begins its attack sensing your weariness from fighting its friends. Its judgment is a poor on, it leaps into the air at you. Your quick reflexes save from certain death, and you strike the creature in its most vulnerable area, its eye. The creature squeals, clicks, and hisses before slowly dying. You sigh with relief that the last of these fearsome spider creatures are finally dead, after a brief rest you continue along the tunnel. After what seems an hour you come to a stop when you notice that the tunnel forks into two different tunnels. One leading upward and the other going downward.

If you wish to take the tunnel leading upward turn to **202.**

If you would rather take the tunnel leading downward turn to **274.**

108

You focus your will on entering the house despite the blaze, and the heat of the flames and the thick back choking smoke fail to hinder your progress. However it is difficult to see, the smoke is as dark as the night sky without a moon and stars. You must feel your way through and use the memory of the layout of the home to guide you to the pleas of your father. You find him the kitchen lying on his back choking on the smoke. Quickly you pull him outside to safety just before the house collapses in on itself. The efforts of this ability have cost you **1** magic point. You turn you father on his side so he can breath better. "Sabin my son…, it is too late for me…., you must find the guild mage. He will know what to do.., hurry my son go!" Are your father's last words as he lies motionless as the cold embrace of death tightens its grip on him. You shed your final tears for both your parents, and shout a curse at the attackers before you set off to find your teacher and guild mage of Lorna.

Turn to **325.**

109

You glance at the guardian ring and focus your mind on reaching your destination; soon you can feel the magic of the ring activating. A soothing breeze washes over you, and the vines that grow around the thorns of the briars begin to shift pointing in the direction that you should take to reach Allendrah. The vines all point in the direction to the tunnel that is directly in front of you. You whisper a thanks to Oak Root once more before walking into the tunnel directly ahead.

Turn to **205.**

110

You calmly breath as you close your eyes and focus on the future of your destiny, if you head east or south you see only pain and death ahead. If you head north you see yourself traveling in circles for weeks and then dying shortly of starvation and madness. Your future looks more promising in the western direction, though the trail is gone that is the safest route to travel. Your mental effort of glimpsing into the future has cost you **2** magic points. You decide to head west, however the terrain will be much more difficult to navigate without the trail. Uneven slopes and forest debris litter the floor.

Turn to **217.**

III

You manage to successfully dodge the burning debris, but the entire roof of the structure will collapse at any moment. You act quickly and manage to find your father; he is covered in black soot and coughing violently. He is lying on his back unable to move, choking you manage to pull your father to safety before the roof claims you both. The strain of your efforts has cost you another health point. You attempt to heal your father's wounds but he is barely even alive. He smiles at you wincing slightly with the strain of breathing, "there isn't much time my son. You... must find the guild mage, quickly before...!" Are your father's last words as the cold embrace of death claims him. You curse those responsible for your parent's fate, and shed your last tears before deciding to honor your father's last wishes. You turn away from your burning home without looking back and head for the guild mages home.

Turn to **325.**

112

You pass the ominous graveyard and continue to look for a decent area in which to rest for the evening, you only walk a few more yards before you find a suitable area with a mostly level forest floor. After you manage to get a campfire started do you relax and gaze upon the strangely overly bright moon, you have never seen it so high in the sky before. The stars too appear much brighter than you have never noticed; it proves to be a little comforting that you can see much better than normal. You must eat a meal or lose **4** health points. The forest is surprisingly calm and serene, so you have no trouble sleeping through the night. When you awaken you restore **2** health points and **1** magic point. The morning is also very relaxing and the terrain for most of your afternoon is also very stable and not difficult to trek along, you notice a single deer and manage to hunt it and harvest its meat, enough for 3 meals. It is not until late in the afternoon before a loud roar from something in the distance freezes you in your tracks. The roar is so loud and low pitched that it makes your stomach churn, you quickly look in all directions for what could make such a terrible sound, but you see nothing?

If you wish to investigate the sound, turn to **214**.

If you would rather remain still where you are turn to **278**.

Or if you possess the ability Enhanced Senses and wish to use them turn to **322.**

113

Quickly and as quietly as you can you turn around and head back to the fork in the tunnel network, you wipe the sweat from your brow and sigh with relief that you are not being followed. The return to the fork brings a new surprise though; you stop before the turn of the corner when you can hear loud clicking and scraping noises. You see two strange large spiders at the fork in the tunnels you were just at, they are green and black. The two strange creatures appear to be half plant and half spider, their thorax's match the thorns and vine textures of the briar's that make up this network of tunnels. They also have one large black cold eye in the center of their heads, and the most fearsome feature of all is the saw like fore arms they possess. They are smaller than you, only about three feet tall. Your heart skips a beat when you suddenly hear clicking noises coming from behind you, the sensation of dread forces you to think quickly.

If you wish to run past the two spider-like creatures and run in the tunnel that leads up turn to **185.**

If you would rather run past the two spider creatures and take the tunnel leading downward turn to 218**.**

If you think it would be more logical to face the upcoming threat turn to **250.**

Or if you possess the ability of Invisibility and wish to use it turn to **294.**

114

You backtrack for almost an hour, but you are not noticing an alternate route. You stop in your tracks and ponder the situation more, your only other option would be to navigate the forest off the trail or go back to the field of toadstool rings.

If you wish to go back and attempt to pass through the toadstool rings turn to **297.**

Or if you would rather take the risk of traveling off the trail turn to **10.**

115

You take the tunnel leading upward, not slowing your pace or looking back you become filled with renewed hope when you can see sunlight poking through the ceiling of the tunnel. You soon feel a gentle breeze blowing in your face; you realize that this tunnel must lead to a way out of here. Excitedly you push your legs to make you run even faster, you are getting close to your goal and you can feel it. Your becomes short lived though when you glance back behind your shoulder and notice an entire horde of spiders barreling down the tunnel towards you, with numbers too many to count in a panic force your body to push on. A frenzy of clicks and hisses shatters your ear drums, your body aches with exhaustion but you know you must escape and succeed in surviving. Soon you can see the end of the tunnel and the bright yellow-orange glow of the sun illuminating the mouth the tunnel, but the sight of something sinister in your path makes you shout a curse. You see a large black spider in front of you; it is different from the others. This one is slightly larger and its forearms are far larger in proportion to its body than the others. The moment the strange creature notices you, it hisses loudly and prepares to attack.

If you possess a bow or crossbow and wish to use it turn to **46.**
If you do not possess either of these weapons and would rather use Spirit-Fire turn to **127.**

If you do not possess either the weaponry, or the special ability turn to **207.**

116

You approach the stranger, his head rises in alarm. He has the appearance of a ruffian, he is dirty and rugged looking with old dirty clothes. The mans blood shot eyes lock onto you with confusion, and before you can ask him about the location of the Azart forest he rises from his seat and runs from the tavern in fear. Confused by the strange mans sudden need to leave you turn your attention back to the front door of the tavern as it suddenly slams open. In walk four men that are dressed in the familiar studded leather vests that were adorned by the attackers of your home. The tattoos of the black dragons on their bare arms make your jaw drop; you figure they must have somehow tracked you from your home to this neighboring village. The barkeeper and other men in the room grow silent as the men walk around the tavern studying everyone inside, you can feel your heart pounding in your chest as you desperately try to formulate a plan of escape.

If you wish to make a run for the door turn to **306.**

If you possess the special ability invisibility and wish to use it turn to **233.**

Or if you would rather wait and see what is going to happen turn to **320.**

117

You quickly in one fluid movement have an arrow readied and pointed at the creatures eye, not letting the sounds of the spider horde behind you distract you from your target you release the bolt. Roll the chance dice.

If you rolled 0-4, turn to **103**.
If you rolled 5 or higher turn to **162.**

118

You turn and run as fast as your legs can carry you through this natural death trap, to your surprise the clicking grows louder and louder. You glance over your shoulder to see the strange half plant half spider creature chasing you. The creature scuttles around the tunnel far quicker than you had thought it would be able to should it put up a chase. It is quickly catching up to you; trying to gain ground on your attacker you push your body even harder. Suddenly the arachnid leaps at you, knocking you to the ground. You go tumbling and rolling on the damp muddy tunnel floor; you recover quickly and are on your feet just in time to avoid the creatures slashing fore arm as it attempts you slice you into two. Weapon ready you must fight this creature to the death.

Briar Arachnid

Attack. 10   Health points. 13
Armor class. 1   Magic points. 0

Hit: 1d4 +3

(This creature is weak to fire, incendiary potions and spirit-fire damage is doubled!)

If you win the combat turn to **195.**

119

At the cost of **2** magic points you quickly call upon the elemental plain for help. Holding your breath as you patiently wait for the assistance of the elementals, you are engulfed in the gas cloud. Your fate is in the hands of the elementals now, soon you notice a powerful breeze spreading across the mushroom field. The thick orange gas is carried high into the sky as the breeze turns into the funnel, but the mushrooms continue to produce more gas. You have a brief moment to escape, and you quickly run to safety. As soon as you are far enough away from the toadstool rings, the caps stop shaking and producing the orange gas. You sigh with relief, and thank the elementals for their timely rescue.

Turn to **348.**

120

With blazing reflexes you have already sent off your first shot, felling one of the foul creatures. The second spider leaps to the ceiling to continue its assault, you already have your second shot lined up and ready. Roll the chance dice.

If you rolled 0-3, turn to **224**.

If you rolled a 4 or higher turn to **279.**

121

You hurriedly leave the dangers of the crypt and the cemetery behind, it is already nightfall and you are tired and hungry. You must eat a meal or lose **4** health points, you mange to find a suitable site for a campfire and to rest for the remainder of the evening. After a brief moment of studying the night sky through the a opening in the forest canopy above your campsite you fall into a deep sleep. Your slumber is undisturbed and you awaken the next morning feeling refreshed, you regain **2** health points and **1** magic point. You begin to wonder how much longer you can take surviving and traveling this treacherous place, you pray that Allendrah is close and your journey will soon come to a close. The sun never breaks through the forest canopy today, and that sets a grim nervous mood for you as you travel. The shadows of the trees dance around tauntingly, and the bird chirping soon comes to a dead silence. The tiny hairs on the back of your neck begin to stand up, and your heart pounds loudly in your chest as you approach a wall of briar patch that stretches as far as the eye can see and well over the trees. You stare at the strange overgrowth with confusion until you spot a single opening just ahead. Like the mouth of a dark cave it beckons to you, and you shrug your shoulders and walk over towards the opening. Realizing that this briar growth covers everything ahead this opening is the only way to progress ahead. Nervously you slowly enter the small mouth of the opening, careful not to get pricked by the thorns of the plant. The floor of what appears to be a tunnel is solid rock, dirt, and thick damp moss. It soon becomes dark like in a cave, (you must use stick and **1** magic point to create a spark to light your way unless you have a torch to spare.) After you have walked several more feet the tunnel forks into three different paths.

If you possess the ability of Fore-Sight and wish to use it turn to **45.**

If you do not possess this ability and would rather use Enhanced- Senses turn to **94.**

If you do not possess either of these abilities, but you have the Guardian ring, turn to **109.**

If you do not possess the guardian ring and would like to take the tunnel leading left turn to **123.**

If you choose to the take the tunnel leading right turn to **161.**

If you would prefer to take the tunnel straight ahead turn to **205.**

122

You sleep through the entire night without further incident, and recover **3** health points, and **2** magic points. The red small embers of the fire you had started are still smoking, and you bury the evidence of having been here in case any bandits are lurking in the area. For hours you trek the open grasslands, the sky is full of white thick clouds, and the sun is as bright and vibrant as ever. Soon you notice something just ahead, there are Hovis herbs growing all over. The tall grass like herb as a mint flavor and the blue green coloration makes it stand out from the grass around it.

If you possess the ability Herbalism and wish to use it turn to **160.**

If you do not possess this ability turn to **313.**

123

Cautiously you trek the left tunnel, the path goes down deep into the darkest parts of this massive network of briar patch. The air becomes humid, and the smell of rotten vegetation fills your nose. Soon you realize that you are heading underground, and now it seems like you are in a sewer. A thin layer of stagnant water lines the muddy floor; vines cover everything as well different types of fungi and moss. All types of insects, worms, and small snakes crawl and slither everywhere around you. The air is so thin that the light from your torch begins to thin and flicker wildly; sweat covers your face as you slowly progress deeper and deeper. Soon the tunnel splits into two paths one leads to the left and the other to the right.

If you wish to head left turn to **238.**

If you choose to go right turn to **329.**

If you have the ability of enhanced senses and wish to use them turn to **33.**

124

The tunnel leading to the right begins to slope upward, and the muddy floor that was once making your progress difficult is not solid dry ground. The tunnel winds and turns abruptly for about a mile, before you can see sunlight coming through the ceiling of the tunnel. You realize that you must closer to escaping this awful place, and your lips form a wide smile on your weathered face. After a sharp turn ahead you stop when you notice that the tunnel once again forks into two different directions, one tunnel leads upward and the other downward.

If you wish to take the tunnel leading upward turn to **41.**

If you choose the tunnel leading downward instead turn to **211.**

125

You reveal the spirit stone to the massive creature; its sunken deep set glowing eyes do not show any signs of interest. The monster grumbles at you loudly, "this is not the spirit stone! It is but an ordinary rock!" You shake your head, and say it only looks like an average rock because you have not managed to awaken its power. The large tree folk glares at you with its skeptical gaze "Be gone with you! Or I shall stomp you into the dirt." It threatens with its booming voice. You growl in frustration, you know you must do something to prove that you are telling the truth.

If you wish to use one of your magical abilities to prove yourself turn to **153.**

Or if you would rather attack the monster, turn to **304.**

126

You are just too weak and exhausted to efficiently fight off any opponents, your quest's difficulties are started to take their toll on your health. You can barely even raise your weapon to defend yourself, and the bandits notice your weakened state and relentlessly attack your horse until it is unable to continue onward. Before you can even realize how critical the situation is you are surrounded by the two bandit horsemen and Falco, still you try to fight off the enemy but to no avail. You are brutally murdered on the road that leads to Balsat.

Your life and quest end here.

127

Still running full speed you extend your open palm at the large black spider monster before you and release a hissing jet of white scorching fire, the briar arachnid screeches as it attempts to resist the burning of your spirit-fire. Your exertion has cost you **1** magic point. You push your way past the flaming enemy without losing ground from the army of spiders that are charging down the tunnel behind you. The end of the tunnel is rapidly approaching, despite the burning sensation of your lungs and legs from severe exhaustion. A glance over shoulder startles you as you notice that horde of spiders are gaining on you, forcing your muscles to push you to your goal you are determined to succeed. It seems like you are moving in slow motion when you step out of the tunnel's mouth and back into the open vastness of the Azart Forest, you take a deep breath. Your relief is quashed when you remember that you are not out of dangers path just yet.

Turn to **187.**

128

As soon as your weapon is drawn and you are ready for combat, the four animals pounce and surround you. You cannot evade the combat and you must them as one enemy.

Wolf Pack

Attack. 38 **Health points. 45**
Armor class. 4 **Magic points. 0**

Hit: 1d20 +3

If your health point total has fallen below **10** Turn to **168.**

If your health point total is above **10** turn to **225.**

129

You nervously reply, "Tameriah." The fae glare at you menacingly, and it is at that moment you realize that you have answered incorrectly. The wrath of these tiny creatures is far worse than you could have possibly thought, a whole new spectrum of pain and agony are how you spend your last moments before you are killed.

Your life and quest end here.

130

The pain of losing everyone you have ever cared about stings you deeply, but you must succeed and not let their deaths be in vain. The most important thing you can do is get the stone back to the elves, and then return home and have your vengeance. You are almost out of Lorna when you notice two of the bandits on horseback just ahead guarding border fence. You stop in your tracks and hide behind a nearby tree, you have to figure out a way to escape unnoticed you will not be able to outrun the enemy when they are on horseback. They are watching the only way out of town, perhaps one of your abilities can present a solution.

If you possess the ability invisibility and wish to use it turn to **255.**

If you do not possess this ability or do not wish to use it, and would rather attempt to sneak past the guards turn to **12.**

Or if you would prefer to take your chances and charge at the enemy in hopes of surprising the horses that they ride on turn to **331.**

131

You tread the tunnel leading in the left direction; it winds and turns abruptly making it more difficult to make progress. The humidity is making your damp clothes stick to your skin uncomfortably, and the thick muddy floor is only getting deeper with every step. You are suddenly startled by a loud clicking noise followed a hiss sound, you freeze in your steps when your eyes catch movement just ahead. You see two large black spiders approaching you; they have abnormally oversized forearms and are larger than any spider you have seen thus far. The pair prepare for an attack, you must defend yourself.

2 Soldier Briar Arachnid's

Attack. 28   **Health points. 36**
Armor class. 2   **Magic points. 0**

Hit: 1d12 +2

(Remember these creatures are weak to fire, incendiary potions and spirit-fire damage is doubled.)

You may evade the combat with these creatures after the first round of combat by turning to **192.**

If you survive the combat turn to **271.**

132

Slowly and cautiously you move in closer and closer to the cooking meat, the closer to the campsite you get the more inviting the scene seems. You still do not notice anything suspicious or anyone around in sight; you are just a couple feet from the campsite when you suddenly feel something tighten around your ankle. A thick rope has tightened around your ankle and the next thing you know you are hanging upside down from a large tree branch, it was a snare trap but who set it? And why? Panicking your eyes dart in every direction you suddenly realize that you are no longer alone. Two large long limbed creatures appear around you with dark green skin, long stringy oily black hair, hairy long bowed legs, and walk upright.

The two monsters are about seven feet tall, with broad long noses, their skin is covered in spots and warts, and they have sunken orange colored eyes. "What have we here Ock?" Grumbles one of the creatures. "It looks like supper Wort." The other reply as it reveals its crooked rotten black teeth as it grins at you. It is then that you realize what these ugly hideous monsters are, trolls! Forest trolls are notorious man eaters, for some reason they only love the flesh of men, women, children, and anything besides the abundant forest life. Your heart sinks as you gaze upon these tall smelly creatures, who managed to create such a clever trap. "I love the taste of travelers Wort; this one will be especially tasty." States Ock with a trail of green drool oozing from his crooked mouth. You must free yourself or you will surely become these monsters next meal.

If you wish to use the ability Spirit- Fire to escape turn to **210**.

If you do not possess this ability and would rather use Elementalism turn to **249**.

If you do not possess either of these abilities, and would rather use your weapon to cut the rope and escape your trap turn to **347**.

133

Your quick reflexes save you from a very disturbing attack, the spider has just secreted a green acidic fluid towards you and when it lands on the ground it immediately burns a steaming hole into the tunnel floor. The spider shrieks loudly in disappointment at its miss, and then takes to the air leaping right for you. Instinctively you strike the large creature in its vulnerable area, its eye. You observe as your weapon bursts the eye of the spider, it hisses and curls into a ball on the ground dead. The two other spiders exchange a series of infuriated clicks and hisses before they attack you.

2 Briar Arachnids

Attack. 20   **Health points. 26**
Armor class. 2   **Magic points. 0**

Hit: 1d8 +3

After you have slain your enemies you waste no time to continue along the tunnel.

Turn to **329.**

134

You continue to run hoping that you will be out of his range with the bow; suddenly you hear the noise of the bow being released. Soon a loud whistling noise fills the air and without warning you feel a very sharp pain in your back, the force of the arrow striking you knocks you to the ground.

Overwhelming pain makes you cry out loudly, you try to stand but then a second bolt strikes you in the chest and kills you instantly.

Your life and quest tragically end here.

135

You take a moment to study your surroundings with your senses, but even with your ability to push your sense of hearing, smell, and the many other advantages that this skill bestows for you it does not help narrow down a safe or even correct route for you to take. You sense danger all around you, and you are now more uneasy and more afraid than ever. You judge that by how the trail ends this is as far as anyone has ever tracked since the trail was even made, you are about to embark in uncharted territory. You swallow a lump in your throat and groan with uncertainty.

If you wish to travel west turn to **333.**
If you would rather travel east turn to **221.**

136

By the time you have slain the soldier arachnid, the spider is upon you. Fighting with all of your might you manage to eliminate many of them, but they're numbers are just too much for you to handle. You are brutally slashed to pieces by hundreds of furiously protective large spiders; you have failed your mission and all of Lamara. The spirit stone remains inside the briar arachnid hive for the rest of time.

Your life and quest end here in the Azart Forest.

137

You close your eyes as you expend **2** magic points, and chant to the elemental plane. After a brief moment of silence the quiet of the chamber is interrupted when a hideous evil voice booms, "You have failed!" You dread what your plea for assistance has brought when the wind begins to pick up carrying sand and searing dirt from the crypt floor all around you. It is then that you realize that this was a mystical test cast by your ancestors to prevent something from being in the hands of evil, and a fearsome torrent of wind covers you. Sand and dirt scrape your face and body relentlessly; you take **1d4** damage. A sinister face appears at the base of the wind funnel, and it smiles malevolently at you with its dark grin and its bright red eyes fill you with fear. Your spell has summoned a powerful evil wind elemental that is intent on destroying you. You must fight to survive.

Dark Elemental (Demon)

Attack. 15   Health points. 30

Armor class. 0   Magic points. 0

Hit: 1d8 +1

(You must reduce your attack by **2** points due to searing sand and dirt hitting your face throughout the combat.

This being is not completely corporeal and is resistant to physical attacks; all physical damage is reduced by half. However this creature is weak to fire, and fire potions, and spirit-fire damage is doubled!) After you have landed the final attack on the creature it screams in agony then dissipates completely from this dimension forever, and the wind around you ceases. Suddenly the crypt entrance door grinds as it slowly opens again revealing a way out of this place.

If you wish to use the ability Necromancy, turn to **77.**

If you choose to use Spirit-Fire instead turn to **228.**

If you do not possess either of these abilities you must leave the crypt by turning to **121.**

138

You hand the three copper coins to the innkeeper, who is all to happy to clutch them into her sweaty wrinkly hands with a toothless smile. You watch as she opens a box to place the currency, then she hurriedly rushes for a rack on the back wall. There are numbers carved into slots with hooks that have some keys hanging from them, "you will stay be in room five." She barks as she hands you the small key. You find your room quickly, and to your dismay it is not to high standard of space or cleanliness. The bed is a small cot, with a large clay pot next to it, the small pillow is dusty and the single blanket on the makeshift bed has small holes and stains on it. You cringe when the dusty old moldy smell of the room invades your nose, beside the bed is an empty crate and there is a wash tub made of copper in a the corner. You decide that is better to sleep indoors than outdoors for the evening. (You must eat a meal or loose **3** health points.) After you are finished looking at the room you lie down on the cot and immediately fall to sleep. However your slumber is interrupted when you hear shouting outside, and commotion from what sounds like a mob of villagers. You immediately spring into action and step out of your room and approach the nearest window that the building has. You notice the entire village gathered by the inn, you gasp in shock by what you see. You see men dressed like the ones that attacked your home circling the throng of people on horseback.

If you possess the ability enhanced senses and wish to use them turn to **198.**

If you do not or would rather not use your intuition turn to **262.**

139

You turn and run, your speed and quick reflexes surprise the two arachnids. They chase you relentlessly along the passage, but just as you are getting exhausted and unable to run any farther they suddenly stop and turn around. With a agitated series of clicks they disappear, confused by their sudden lax of pursing you. You shrug your shoulders and dismiss the encounter. The tunnel soon splits into two different passages that go in different directions, one leads upward and the other downward.

If you wish to go upward turn to **41.**

If you choose to go downward instead turn to **211.**

140

At the cost of **2** magic points you concentration on the image of the future that has suddenly appeared in your minds eye. You see a myriad of half spider half plant creatures that dwell here, in fact your insight informs you that this is not completely a natural occurrence with plant life. This is in fact a large Briar arachnid nest, an ancient spider of unknown origin. Created by a powerful life form, it has adapted perfectly for life in the Azart Forest. They are roughly three feet tall, green and black. They have a single black eye on their head that has excellent vision, and possess saw like forearms for slashing prey and creating tunnels out of the briar bush they live in. They also secrete a very powerful acidic fluid that can melt even the most durable metals and shields. You shudder at what you have just seen, but you must reach the exit of this nest if you are to reach Allendrah.

Turn to **204.**

141

After what seems an eternity you force yourself free from the rock and push against the current that is trying to keep you on the river bottom. Your first breath of fresh air is so sweet and refreshing, but even though you are at the surface of the water you are not out of danger yet. The current carries you farther downstream and you are violently smacked against several more rocks, dealing **1d8** damage to you. After several more long moments of fighting the powerful current you manage to pull yourself to the shore of the other side of the river bank. Completely out of strength you lay on the gravel shore of the bank resting, you lose another health point. After you are recovered enough to stand, walk along the bank until you manage to find the other side of the trail.

Turn to **4.**

142

The soldier briar arachnid topples over one last wailing squeal as it dies; you sigh with relief and continue for the end of the tunnel. You can see bright sunlight shining inside the mouth of the exit, just imagining the fresh outside air and atmosphere makes you yearn for the safety of the forest. Your hopes however soon become dashed when you can hear loud clicks, hissing, and screeching noises coming from behind you. A glance over your shoulder makes you shudder with fear, a horde of briar arachnids is charging towards you. Disturbing this normally docile nest has provoked an attack from the entire hive; you force your aching legs to carry you towards your goal. It seems like your arrival at the end of this long dreadful tunnel is coming in slowing motion, but the moment you set foot back into the Azart Forest you feel instant relief. You are still not out of harms way though!

Turn to **187.**

143

After using **2** magic points you ritually chant in a whisper for the aid of the elementals, after a few moments you wait for the answer to your call to be heard. Suddenly your attention is drawn to one of the burning buildings, you watch as the fire grows and roars loudly. A single ball of flames leaps out onto the ground without warning and takes on a more humanoid form; it sprouts a head, arms, and legs. The bandits observe in fear, as a fire elemental charges at them. They desperately try to fend off the fiery beast, but to no avail. The fire elemental has already claimed three victims; the villagers use this opportunity to take on the other bandits alongside the elemental. You seize your opportunity to make a run for it; you slip past the scene unnoticed. But as you turn past the next building you hear shouts in the distance, you notice two more bandits ahead trying to prevent your escape.

Turn to **6.**

144

You carefully place the key into the hole and turn it clockwise, there is a very loud click and without warning the stairs that lead to the first floor of the crypt retract and the door begins to close. You become fearful that you have set off another trap, and with your weapon ready you prepare for whatever threat your ancestors have set before you. Suddenly the remains of the skeletons begin to tremble and reassemble into skeletal warriors; you have never seen such a frightening visage before. The sound of old aged cracked bones re-attaching to their once complete bodies is chilling and unsettling, but before you can think of a way out you are surrounded by the undead. Re-animated by a level of necromancy far beyond your current skill level these mindless servants of an ancient spell descend upon you. You cannot evade this fight you must these skeleton warriors off.

Skeleton warriors (Undead)

Attack. 20   **Health points. 30**

Armor class. 5   **Magic points. 0**

Hit: 1d6 +5

After you land the final assault on the last skeleton its bones explode into shards and dust like the rest of its kin, you sigh with relief that you have conquered the host of the undead. After you have rested enough you hear the fire from the center of the room begin to grow. It crackles and hisses loudly as a wall of fire appears before, and suddenly a humanoid form appears before you. It is a spirit surrounded in ancient magic, and judging by its clothes it is not hostile. You recognize the riven mage symbol on its transparent tunic, the image of Ulzar smiles at you warmly. "You have managed to pass every test that we have placed inside this enchanted tomb; you have proven yourself worthy of the riven clan secret." The voice of Ulzar echoes. Suddenly another chamber opens just on the other side of the room, you watch as the form of Ulzar disappears and the roaring fire returns to normal.

Turn to **246.**

Despite the impending doom that is about to set upon you, you chant to the elemental plain and channel the energy spent into the spirit stone. Without warning your hand begins to tremble as the rock begins to glow with a milky white glow, and a surge of unfathomable power is surrounding you. At the cost of **50** magic points, (You do not need to subtract any points from your magic total.) The very wind that surrounds begins to pick up, the granite and dirt below your feet tremble, and the heat from your hands turns into a raging red flame. With your mouth agape in awe you have an elemental of every type of element before you, a large clay golem stands in front of you, a fire elemental appears and floats before you, a wind elemental taking the form of a tornado surrounds you, and a water elemental rises from a cloud of vapor next to you. They all look at you patiently awaiting your command, "Destroy!" You command as you extend your finger at the approaching spider horde.

Suddenly the most amazing spectacle is laid before you, as the elementals spring into offensive action. Even with numbers well into the hundreds the spiders are no match for these super natural beings, and despite certain advantages one elemental would have against another they work together in perfect harmony as they dispatch the arachnids. It does not take long before every single briar arachnid is slain; a field of eight-legged corpses surrounds you. The elementals approach you, "The monsters are slain, we must go." They say simultaneously. You thank them and nod, and just as quickly as they were summoned they are gone. (Restore all lost health points and magic points to their original level.) The spirit stones bright glow now dims, at last you have the mighty vessel of the spirit stone awakened and you can now find Allendrah. Just as you begin to set off something new catches your eye.

Turn to **241.**

146

The farther you walk into the darkness of this strange alien forest, the colder your skin gets. The only sound you can hear is that of the small invisible wildlife such as birds, and squirrels. The forest has a strong dirt like odor to it, and the trees are so tall and thick the suns light can barely break through the dense canopy. You recall the many tales of the different monsters and beguiling enchantments of this ancient forest. Your father had told you that long ago this forest used to stretch clear to the border of your home village, and it was once a lush paradise. But after man took his axes to the trees, the forest grew vengeful and cursed. Your father also told you that was when the Elves of Allendrah became detached from the people of your home, you hope that your visit here with the spirit stone will re-kindle that once prominent relationship with man and the forest. You know that you must also solve the mystery of the spirit stone and get its power to re-awaken so that you can find the fabled city of the elves. After hours of long walking along the overgrown trail you begin to get the feeling that you are being watched. The tiny hairs on the back of your neck begin to stand up; you suddenly stop in your tracks.

If you possess the ability of enhanced senses and wish to use them turn to **244.**

If you do not possess this ability turn to **40.**

147

You release your bolt; it flies into Falco's chest. He pauses and removes the shaft from his ribcage, and glares at you. "Foolish boy, arrows are not going to stop me." Laughs the bandit leader as he prepares to charge again.

If you wish to fire another shot and aim for his head turn to **89.**

If you wish to fire another shot and aim for the heart turn to **259.**

If you would rather use the spirit stone turn to **51.**

If you would rather use the ability fore-sight to discover the means of his supernatural abilities turn to **177.**

If you do not possess this ability or do not wish to use it and would rather use elementalism to deal with this threat turn to **287.**

148

At the cost of **2** magic points you close your eyes and focus on a very brief view of the future if you were to intrude on this mysterious campsite. Soon a horrible image appears in your minds eye, two hideous creatures that lurk deep in these woods set traps for unsuspecting travelers such as yourself to devour. They are tall green, and by all means very dangerous. Though this campsite seems harmless, there is a snare trap rigged somewhere towards the campfire.

If you wish to ignore the campsite and continue your quest, turn to **318.**

If you would rather take your chances and investigate the campsite, turn to **132.**

149

You meet the bandit lord's fury in a series of blows exchanged between the two of you; the battle is full of intensity as you attempt to bring the man down for good. Your attacks are damaging but do not seem to sap the man of his unnatural means of power and strength, and before too long you are to weak and wounded to fight back and are quickly overpowered. Falco wastes no time in cutting your neck open with demonic weapons and death is quick.

You have allowed the world of Lamara to sink into the grip of an unstoppable evil, your quest tragically ends here.

150

At the cost of **2** magic points, you calmly close your eyes despite the current disaster and focus your powers into a brief glimpse of the past. Your minds eye has placed the image of a black dragon, it is the symbol of evil and all your people have been warned of. You also see a far away frigid land of the north, and a fleet of dark vessels sailing the oceans. An overpowering sensation of fear, anger, and hatred brings you to your knees. You force yourself from your trance and realize that your home is under attack, and you must do what you can to save anyone left. Your thoughts soon turn to your family, and immediately you run towards your farmhouse in hopes that your parents are unharmed.

Turn to **300.**

151

Unable to elude your attackers you stand ready for combat, the troll duo seems eager to strike you down for their supper.

Trolls

Attack. 26   Health points. 34
Armor class. 2   Magic points. 0

Hit: 1d10 +3

After both of the large lumbering trolls fall to the ground dead, you only find two copper coins and the club that one carried. (If you want to keep the club it has the same item benefits that # 3 mace has on the weapons list for you to refer to.) You do not hesitate to flee the troll encampment.

Turn to **3.**

152

Your enhanced senses detect a disturbance in the wind, and that something is coming straight for you. You only have seconds to react to the unseen attack. Roll the chance dice.

If you rolled 0-2, turn to **197.**
If you rolled a 3 or higher turn to **243.**

153

The choice is yours of which ability would best prove your case to this omnipotent being, but remember choose wisely.

If you wish to use the ability Spirit-Fire, turn to **191**.
If you choose to use Elementalism instead turn to **52.**
Or if you would rather use Necromancy turn to **200.**
Or if you prefer to use the ability Invisibility, turn to **302.**

154

With the mighty spirit stone held tightly in your hands, you pour all of your energy into the stone and channel it. (This has cost you all of your magic points.) The stone surges with enough power to create a beam of pure power that is blasted at Falco, he stops dead in his tracks with a terrified expression on his evil face. "This is not possible; I cannot be bested by a mere child….NOOOOO!" Shouts the panicked bandit leader the dark force that was imbued to his being is forced back to the realm from wince it came. You watch as reality sets in for Falco and the light of the spirit stone dims, you can sense his heart slowly beating. He collapses on the ground trembling and gurgling, you peer over your mortal enemy. You see the faces of your family and people as you stare into their murderer's eyes, "This is for my family and mentor!" You whisper as you deliver a merciful but deadly strike to his middle finishing him off once and for all. You have at last avenged your people and have slain the bandit leader.

Turn to **53.**

155

You cannot believe that you are actually riding a horse for the first time, the powerful animal moves with such speed. As you glance back behind your shoulder, you notice two bandit riders closing in at each side and the leader right behind them. You glance out at the darkness of night ahead, the full moon and stars that cover the sky provide little light you cannot see very far ahead. You realize that you need to loose them; you are no match for three bandit horsemen. For now you decide it is best to remain on the main road, you do not know what kind of dangers lurk in the tall grass of the Lorna Grasslands. You desperately search all over with your eyes for some means of escaping this threat; you notice a wooden sign ahead that reads:

Lark's Bluff →E 25 miles
Balsat ← W 30 miles

If you wish to head east to Lark's Bluff turn to **293.**
Or if you would rather head west to Balsat turn to **50.**

156

You pour every last reserve of energy you can give to the spirit stone, a tremendous bolt of power pushes the evil shadowy power given to Falco from his body revealing the empty shell that he really is. And now that the demonic force is no longer a part of him, the wounds he sustained from this reality are setting in. He drops to his knees with the look of panic and terror on his pale face, "NOOOO… this cannot be. Bested by a mere child…" You watch as he falls over onto his back, his death is coming. Holding back tears in memory of what this man did to your family and people you slowly approach his dying body. "This is for my family, and mentor." You say full of anger and deliver the killing blow to the bandit master.

Turn to **53.**

157

You bat the briar arachnid back a couple of feet with your weapon before you turn and run, you can hear the clicking noises of your attacker directly behind you as you flee. As you run can hear more clicking noises and it is then that you notice two more briar arachnids ahead climbing the walls. They immediately notice you and leap to the floor to intercept you, holding your breath you sidestep a slashing fore arm that swings in your direction then you manage to jump over the seconds attacking arm. Before you know it you are surrounding by three clicking spiders as the one that was chasing you leaps over its comrades and lands in front of you. You must fight all three of these as one enemy.

3 Briar Arachnids

Attack. 24	**Health points. 28**
Armor class. 3	**Magic points. 0**

Hit: 1d12 +1

If you survive the fight, turn to **235**.

158

You turn and run full speed, and with a loud ear shattering howl the lone wolf pursues you. It is much more difficult to evade such a beast in the dark with no trail to ease your escape, you almost trip over a rock but you manage to remain upright. This gives the wolf the time it needs to catch up to and you scream in pain when you feel its sharp fangs sink into your calve muscle. You lose **2** health points; the smell of your blood has attracted the attention of four more wolves. The rest of the pack is in a blood frenzy, and you are unable to run any further. You quickly prepare for the fight of your life, you cannot evade this fight.

Wolf pack

Attack. 38	**Health points. 45**
Armor class. 4	**Magic points. 0**

Hit: 1d20 +3

If your health point total has fallen below **10** Turn to **168**.

If your health point total is above **10** turn to **225**.

159

With the use of another magic point you hurl a jet of scorching white flames at the spider duo, both scream and hiss as they burn to death before you. The stench of charred spider makes you cough, but you sigh with relief before continuing along the tunnel. After a long period of constant abrupt turns and downhill and uphill trekking you arrive at a split in the tunnel, there is a tunnel going upward and the other downward.

If you wish to take the tunnel leading upward turn to **41.**

If you would prefer to take the tunnel going downward, turn to **211.**

160

You can use this rare hovis herb to create antidote potions, and you immediately pick the surprisingly tough grass like plant and your pestle and mortar. You grind the blades of the leaves into a paste like substance, and sample the flavor to make sure that it is ripe enough for use. The flavor is good, and sweet. (If you wish to keep any of the hovis, there is enough to make up to 3 antidote potions.) After you are finished making the necessary potions that you require you place your equipment back into your backpack.

Turn to **313.**

161

The right tunnel proves a challenge to trek, the terrain is never level and it winds and turns as well as goes uphill abruptly and downhill all at once, the dim lighting makes it difficult to see random leaf litter and debris so you almost trip every few feet that you walk. The air is humid, and the smell is musky. You get the feeling that a monster will appear around a corner at any moment, but you manage to shake your nerves in hopes of reaching your destination soon. You force yourself to remain as far away from the walls as possible, since it is only thorny briars and vines that make the foundation of this tunnel. Suddenly you reach a fork in your path; there is a tunnel leading upwards and the other downwards.

If you wish to take the tunnel going upwards turn to **202.**

If you choose the tunnel leading downward turn to **274.**

If you possess the ability of Enhanced- Senses and wish to use them turn to **344.**

162

You release your bolt, it sails true right into the spiders eye. There is a loud popping noise as the shaft and tip of the bolt rupture the eye, and the arachnid screeches loudly then drops to the ground dead. You sigh with relief in your accuracy, but you must escape this tunnel before the spider horde behind you catches up to you. Your legs burn with exhaustion, your heart beats and pounds painfully in your chest but you are determined to escape and succeed in your mission. The end of the tunnel is rapidly approaching, and you feel instant relief when you set foot back outside the Azart Forest. The fresh air soothes your senses and the sunlight makes you smile widely, but you are not out of dangers path just yet.

Turn to **187.**

163

The remainder of the day is uneventful; you do not see anymore strange beings or threatening monsters of any kind. You do manage to hunt a couple of squirrels enough to have for a meal, and you make a campsite close to the trail. You fall asleep staring up at the dark canopy of the forest; you awaken the next morning feeling very refreshed. You regain **3** health points and **1** magic point. The morning however the forest is covered in a thick layer of gray fog. You decide to use the last bit of flame from your campfire to light a torch to help navigate the trail. After hours of walking slowly through the thick fog, you can suddenly hear the sound of running water just ahead. That tells you that you are heading closer towards the Infernal Bog just north of the Azart Forest. The waterways run from the swamp, you can soon see the bank of a river in the distance. You stop at the bank and survey the current of the water, the rapids from the river water seem really powerful and there is no bridge in which to cross to the trail on the other side. You will have to either attempt to cross the dangerous rapids or you can go downstream and search for a more shallow area to cross the river.

If you wish to cross the river here directly to the other side of the trail, turn to **206**.

Or if you would rather try to cross the river further downstream turn to **272.**

164

Your mouth is agape at what you notice shambling towards you making loud clicking noises; it is a large spider-like creature that is part plant also. It is about three feet tall, dark green and black coloration. It has a single large black cold eye in the center of its large head, and it has two saw lick fore arms and has a pulsating abdomen. With your weapon ready you attack the strange creature; it seems surprised by your sneak attack but is quick to defend itself.

Briar Arachnid

Attack. 10   **Health points. 13**
Armor class. 1   **Magic points. 0**

Hit: 1d4 +3

(This creature is weak to fire, incendiary potions and spirit-fire damage is doubled!)

If you survive the combat turn to **195.**

165

Losing all sense of direction you are still unable to find the trail before nightfall, feeling extremely panicked you lose a nights sleep. You attempt to use local lore from your village to try and use land marks and moss growth direction to find your way, but you are becoming more and more lost in this maze of a forest. Soon more and more days pass, and you are unable to find any food to gather or hunt.

You become destined to wander the Azart Forest until

you slowly die from starvation and madness, you life and quest end here.

166

You awaken early the next morning restoring **4** health points, and **2** magic points. The loud chirping of the large variety of song birds gives you the motivation to enjoy the daylight hours of the forest more than the night hours. You quickly put out the remaining embers of your campfire and gather your belongings, and then you locate the trail and continue your journey. The hours fly by and you constantly watch over your shoulders to make sure that your not being followed or hunted by any unseen threats. However late afternoon you stop in your tracks as you notice a stretch of large mushrooms growing in a circular pattern all over the trail and as far as you can see ahead. These strange mushrooms are almost up to your waist and the wide yellow and white caps glisten with some kind of resin all over the edges. You are not sure if this plant life is entirely safe to pass through, you have never seen toadstool rings like these before?

If you possess the ability Herbalism and wish to use it to attempt to identify the wild toadstool rings turn to **258.**

If you wish to pass through the toadstool rings and continue on the trail turn to **297.**

Or if you would rather back track the trail and find an alternate means of getting to Allendrah turn to **28.**

167

They seem to love attack you in small clusters ranging from three to six at a time, you easily cut them down. Soon there are only a couple of the small spiders left, they eventually give up on trying to take you down and leave. You wipe several beads of sweat from your damp forehead, and sigh loudly with relief. You press on farther down the long eerie tunnel without any more disturbances, until the tunnel splits into two different directions. One tunnel leads upward, and the other downward.

If you wish to take the tunnel leading upward turn to **41.**

Or if you would rather follow the tunnel leading downward turn to **211.**

168

As hard as you try to fight off the vicious wolf pack, they are just too much for you to handle. When you focus your attacks on one or two of them, a third wolf manages to strike you. You suddenly notice how wounded you really are when you cannot even lift your weapon any longer to defend yourself. The wolf pack does not waste any time to rend you to pieces and begin eating you alive.

Your life and quest tragically end here in the Azart Forest!

169

With a fluid motion you have your weapon aimed and ready to fire. You must roll the chance dice.

If you rolled 0-3, turn to **229.**
If you rolled 4 or higher turn to **281.**

170

At the cost of **3** magic points you close your eyes, and allow the magic to slip into everyone's blind spot. The enemy will be unable to see you, but that does not make you completely undetectable. You must be careful and use patience to slip past these men before the incantation wares off, there is not much time so after you are unable to see your body you slowly step out into the open and begin to walk towards the path just ahead. So far the enemy and everyone around you is totally oblivious to your presence, it is only moments after you reach the trail that the spell begins to ware off and you quickly stick to the shadows. It is not long before you find the well hidden and undisturbed shack of the guild mage, on the very outskirts of the village this small hut is made from the remains of a giant trunk of an ancient tree that once lived in Lamara so long ago. You begin to feel relieved that the elder has not been discovered, for he will surely know what to do.

Turn to **90**.

171

The large arachnid hisses loudly before doubling over dead, you sigh with relief and waste to time to continue along the tunnel. Your trek becomes more and more difficult, the muddy ground on which you walk gets deeper and stickier the more travel. To make matters worse you notice two more arachnids approaching you, they are crawling on the ceiling and moving towards you at frightening speed. They hiss and click as they begin their assault, you must act quickly if you are to survive.

If you possess a bow or crossbow and wish to use it turn to **245.**

If you do not have these weapons, but possess the ability Spirit-Fire and wish to use it turn to **285.**

If you do not possess either of these weapons, or skills but have the power of elementalism and would like to call upon the elementals for assistance turn to **317.**

If you do not possess such weaponry, or either of these abilities you must prepare for combat by turning to **22.**

172

At the cost of **2** magic points you close your eyes for a glimpse of the future if you were to set foot inside this scary graveyard, and to your alarm there is an old evil force that resides inside somewhere waiting for unsuspecting travelers to pass through. But your keen insight also informs you of an unseen treasure of some sort?

If you wish to risk the danger and enter the graveyard, turn to **70.**

Or if it is too dangerous and you choose to journey away from the graveyard turn to **112.**

173

Still running full speed you extend your open palm at the large black spider monster before you and release a hissing jet of white scorching fire, the briar arachnid screeches as it attempts to resist the burning of your spirit-fire. Your exertion has cost you **1** magic point. You push your way past the flaming enemy without losing ground from the army of spiders that are charging down the tunnel behind you. The end of the tunnel is rapidly approaching, despite the burning sensation of your lungs and legs from severe exhaustion. A glance over shoulder startles you as you notice that horde of spiders are gaining on you, forcing your muscles to push you to your goal you are determined to succeed. It seems like you are moving in slow motion when you step out of the tunnel's mouth and back into the open vastness of the Azart Forest, you take a deep breath. Your relief is quashed when you remember that you are not out of dangers path just yet.

Turn to **187.**

174

Your steed is becoming exhausted, and when you feel it is safe to so you pull from the trail to allow your horse to rest. You soon realize that you are starving; you must heat one meal or lose **4** health points. Your clash with the bandits and the leader has left you exhausted, after a moment of setting up a fire you drift off to sleep. The rest of your night is not disturbed, the bandits have either given up their pursuit of you or they are unable to track you. You feel refreshed and rested; you restore **3** health points and **2** magic points. After you let your horse feed on some of the grass you continue your quest, the sun is high in the cloudless sky. A cool soothing breeze relaxes your nervous as you constantly look over your shoulder for signs of being followed. Hours fly by without incident, and by late afternoon you arrive at Lark's Bluff. You can see in the distance the trees that you assume line up to make the Azart Forest. The dirt path has a fork in the path with a trail that goes left, and another that goes right.

If you wish to take the left path turn to **237.**

Or if you would rather take the path that goes to the right turn to **307.**

If you possess the ability of enhanced senses and wish to use it turn to **15.**

175

The tunnel takes a sharp right, and winds abruptly making it difficult to prepare any dangers that may be lurking around the corner. After a short moment, you notice something useful growing near a muddy pool on the tunnel floor. There is a cluster of small white glowing mushrooms growing, you immediately recognize as they luminari mushrooms. They have two beneficial properties, the first being that they can glow in the dark creating a small light source. And they also have healing benefits, (If you possess the ability Herbalism, you may pick enough for two vials. These mushrooms restore **3** health points, and you no longer would have to use a torch to light your way through the dark. If you do not possess the special ability Herbalism, you may take one cluster of these mushrooms for consumption right now. Or to use as a torch.) Soon the tunnel begins to slope downwards more before coming to another split, there is a tunnel leading upward, and the other downward.

If you wish to take the tunnel leading upward turn to **202.**

If you prefer to the tunnel going downward turn to **274.**

176

You tell the large tree like being that you are just an innocent passerby, with no interest other than reaching the end of the forest. The massive being stares at you intensely with its sunken green lantern eyes skeptically, then points its large branch like arm at you. "You lie! There have not been travelers that have come this far for any reason other than to reach the end of the forest. Your deceit will be your undoing agent of evil, for too has your kind come here to cut down my sanctuary. We have protected man and sheltered man, and what does your kind do in return? They take their axes to our trees and break the sacred rites of the forest. Be gone foul deceiver! Away with you!" Booms the tree's low rumbling voice as it blocks the path thus preventing you progress in your quest.

If you wish to attack this being, turn to **304**.

Of if you would rather tell the tree folk the truth turn to **68.**

177

At the cost of **2** magic points, you are immediately pulled into a trance like state where time seems to stop while your minds eye glimpses into the past. You see a frozen wasteland and a single civilization on the brink of extinction. Two strange beings arrive on a large vessel covered only in black robes, and their faces hidden by the oversized hoods. You notice Falco being selected for some type of strange evil ritual in which his soul is exchanged for a demonic influence that gives him unnatural power, and it suddenly becomes obvious of how to rid him of his evil intent and set in the laws of nature back in balance. You must use the power of the spirit stone on him to allow him to die from his wounds and reverse the effects of the evil transference with his soul.

Continue, by turning to **51.**

178

One of the bandits notices you and immediately begins to charge with his horse, and then the second begins to follow. The horses move with alarming speed and you are unable to avoid the first bandit, as he draws his weapon and shouts a battle cry. (Subtract 1 point from your attack rating, due to the enemy being on horseback.) (This combat will only last one round before the second rider arrives!)

Bandit horseman

Attack. 13   **Health 1points. 15**
Armor class. 2   **Magic points. 0**

Hit: 1d6 +1

You may avoid the combat after one round before the second rider appears by turning to **288.**

Or if you would rather fight them both turn to **55.**

179

At the cost of **2** magic points, your minds eye allows you to see a projectile attack in the works. You are the primary target of your mysterious attacker.

Continue, by turning to **243.**

180

With the expense of **3** magic points you softly chant the incantation of the spell, and your body slips into the ether just in time. The two menacingly ugly ogre like trolls break through a large briar patch just a few feet ahead of you, both sniffing the air with they're large long stubby snouts trying to seek you out. You remain completely still and completely invisible to their eyes, and slowly they creep closer and closer. You can hear your heart beating loudly in your chest as you pray that your ruse works and that they give up the chase soon. "I smell the fleshy one close by Ock!" Barks the troll closest to you sticking his nose in the air high. You realize that if they can't find you by eye-sight that they will find you by your scent. Looking around frantically for an escape route you notice a thick patch of bushes that you can creep to and escape, or you can just run for it and hope they do not notice you. You do not have much time to act; your spell will wear off any moment.

If you wish to sneak over towards the bushes turn to **282.**

If you choose to run for it turn to **332.**

181

As the two large black hissing arachnids approach, you already manage to prepare your weapon and take aim. You must roll the chance dice.

If you rolled 0-4, turn to **231.**
If you rolled 5 or higher turn to **291.**

182

You turn and run as fast as you can from the wolf, it howls again more horribly than the first time and chases after you. The large beast is faster than you had anticipated; you can hear its sharp teeth's clattering together as it tries to bite your leg. You come to sudden halt when two more large wolf's jump out in front of you teeth showing, you cannot hope to outrun these apex predators and must fight for your life.

3 large wolves

Attack. 24   **Health points. 36**

Armor class. 3   **Magic points. 0**

Hit: 1d10 +3

If you survive the combat turn to **251.**

183

You take aim, with pure skill and accuracy you release the bolt. It sails into Falco's chest, he is knocked back a step and gasps for air. The bandit master glares at you and laughs, "Is this the best you can do?" He taunts and removes the shaft from his rib cage. You curse your misfortune, and sling your bow/ crossbow over your shoulder as Falco charges towards you and attacks with his daggers in each hand. You defend yourself and fight valiantly, but you reach the point of exhaustion quickly as you realize that you are not going to be able to kill this man. Before you can even think of a way to strip him of his supernatural powers he has overpowered you and slit your throat, you die quickly by the venomous powers of his demonic weaponry.

You have failed, your life and quest end here.

184

The troll swings his club with all of his strength, and you managed to use your body weight to swing yourself out of striking range. You manage to use the smooth fluid motions of your movement to swing your body up high enough to cut the rope that binds you in the air upside down and free yourself. You land hard on the ground taking **1** damage. Before you can stand the troll is taking another swing at you with its club, and you parry the attack with your weapon. The second troll growls loudly and joins his comrade for combat, you cannot escape this fight.

Trolls

Attack. 26	**Health points. 34**
Armor class. 2	**Magic points. 0**

Hit: 1d10 +3

After both of the large lumbering trolls fall to the ground dead, you only find two copper coins and the club that one carried. (If you want to keep the club it has the same item benefits that # 3 mace has on the weapons list for you to refer to.) You do not hesitate to flee the troll encampment.

Turn to **3**.

185

You quickly dash past the two arachnid's, they make loud alarmed clicking noises then begin to chase you in the tunnel going upward. You dare not look back at the pursuing threat; you force your legs to move you faster and faster up the steep uphill tunnel. The terrain is much easier on your feet the higher the tunnel goes, but you can hear by the increase in the number of clicking noises that there is even more activity all around you. As if an entire horde of bee's have been disturbed your ears fill with an ear shattering clicking noises coming from all over the entire briar and vine structure. Soon you approach another fork in the tunnels; there is a left and right tunnel. You must decide quickly before the entire host of briar arachnids is upon you.

If you wish to take the left tunnel turn to **277.**
If you choose the right tunnel instead turn to **343.**

186

When you approach the three men you discover that they are playing cards, and you invited to play with them. (If you wish to decline their offer and would rather talk to the lone stranger turn to **116.**) If not continue. The three men are travelers from the port city Dhax just north of here, when you inquire about the Azart forest they eye you with concern. The man that calls himself Dale is a middle aged pot bellied peddler that grabs your shoulder roughly. "Why in the world would you want to travel that horrid place, it is cursed boy?" You swallow a lump in your throat, and you explain that you must find it without revealing the nature of your quest. Dale laughs at you but decides to answer your question. "Two days east from here you will find a fork at Lark's bluff, if you take the path to the right it will take you to the Azart forest, but if you take the path to the left you will be heading down bandit road. Rightly called so because it has been taken over by thieves and various criminals."

You thank Dale for the information. Before you can leave you are talked into one game with these men, you reluctantly accept and the buy in per round after the first game is one copper. (Here are the rules for the card game: Roll the d20 dice, and then try to roll under the value with a d10. If a 1-5 is rolled with the d20 re-roll the dice, for every time you roll under the value you win 4 copper, but if you bet more then 1 copper your bet is matched and you multiply the number of winnings by the amount you bet. If you loose the bet that is how much copper you loose. You can play as many rounds of cards as you wish.)

If you decide you want to visit the herbalist shop turn to **102.**
Or if you would rather visit the smithy, turn to **208.**
Or if you would rather remain in the tavern turn to **339.**

187

You watch in horror as the wave of arachnid's pour from the tunnel that you just exited, like a nest of angry army ants they amass in a relentless wave against you. Running, you desperately ponder a means of escaping this wave of monsters that will be on top of you soon. Panic floods your mind as you are unable to notice a way out of this problem;

you curse your rotten luck. You cannot believe that you have made it this far to Allendrah to be killed by a legion of arachnids, you feel like you have failed your people and the secrets of the Riven clan will die with you and the rest of Lamara. Never before have you needed your mentors guidance and reassurance so badly; you tried your hardest to succeed in such over whelming odds. And just as you are about to accept your tragic fate, you hear a familiar voice that not only startles you but warms your mood.

It is the voice of your mentor, but how? You wonder and you take the opportunity to listen to the voice. "You must awaken the power of the Spirit Stone Sabin! You must re-light the spark of its magic now!" Echoes the voice of your mentor. You cannot see him anywhere, but you can sense his presence as if he were running through the forest with you. "But how?" You ask, full of confusion. "You must use magic Sabin, only the magic of what I have taught you can re-activate the stone. It is your destiny to use the stone, hurry." Pleads the echoing voice of your mentor across the spirit world. You suddenly feel the urge to remove the stone from your backpack, it still has the appearance of an ordinary gray rock but you realize that you must use one of your spells correctly to awaken the powers of this artifact to save your life.

If you choose the ability of Spirit-Fire to invoke the stone, turn to **24.**

If you choose the ability of Tolerance, turn to **71.**

If you choose to invoke the stone with the ability of Elementalism turn to **145.**

If you choose the ability Invisibility, turn to **216.**

If you choose to invoke the stone with Necromancy turn to **248.**

If you would rather use the ability of Fore-Sight turn to **273.**

If you wish to use Curing instead to invoke with the stone turn to **311.**

If you do not have any magic points left and your health point total has fallen below **10,** turn to 336.

If you do not have any magic points left and your health point total is above **10,** turn to **341.**

188

You follow the direction of the arrow on the owl statue, to your surprise a vibrant green moss trail appears before you to follow. The mystical forces that comprise this forest never cease to amaze you, when you think that you have figured everything out about this place something new presents itself. You have the feeling that you are back on track to your destination when the moss trail ends and you do not have that eerie feeling that you are heading in the wrong direction.

Turn to **3.**

189

After you have slain the spider, its two comrades hiss at you viciously. You prepare for another attack, but they only click and turn around and scurry away hurriedly. You shrug your shoulders relieved that you did not have to worry about two more of these awful monsters attacking you. You slowly continue along the tunnel, the foul smell of rotted vegetation and muddy slime makes you nauseous. After a sharp turn the tunnel splits into two different directions, one tunnel leads upward and the other downward.

If you wish to take the tunnel leading upward turn to **41.**

If you choose the tunnel going downward instead turn to **211.**

190

Without warning you stumble over a loose rock on the ground, you roll onto your knees. The sting from the fall does not slow you down much, but the pursuing bandits have managed to gain the ground they need to engage you in combat. You manage to put up a good fight, but your lack of combat experience has left you unable to fight off more than one enemy and you are violently slain where you stand.

Your life and quest end here.

191

You calmly open your right palm, and soon after pointing it up the air the temperature begins to rise rapidly. The tree folk watches with interest as white fire appears in your palm and you send a searing jet of spirit-fire into the sky; the flames hiss like a snake and clap in the air like a bolt of crackling lightning. Your effort has cost you **1** magic point. The large hulking being has its uneven large mouth agape in astonishment, "The flames of the spirit! Only a Riven mage or Elf can do that." The tree's low rumbling voice echoes loudly. You nod, "Indeed you are truthful. But how can this be, the riven clan has all but died out long ago?" You shake your head and in great detail explain how it is that you have come in possession of the spirit stone and why you seek the elves of Allendrah. "I am called Oak Root, the guardian of the Azart Forest. Long have my kin populated the trees of this forest, but still the forest shrinks and continues to die?" Booms the tree folk's loud voice in frustration. You lower your head in sorrow, "I am sorry that man no longer respects the forest."

Oak Root smiles at you warmly, "The elves of Allendrah have remained hidden and unseen in their sacred garden for many centuries. Care not do they for the well being of the forest, I have begged for them to intervene but they never leave the garden to help the forest. I will help as best I can …?" "Sabin!" You say as you interrupt the giant. "Sabin… I will help you, but you must accompany me to our domain." Beckons Oak Root. "Our Domain?" You ask full of confusion. Oak Root opens his branch like arms wide and it is then that you notice the other tree folk creatures all around you. They all vary in appearance no two of these massive giants look alike. You count at least five others walking closer towards you and Oak Root.

"They have come to see the last of the Riven clan." States Oak Root as he greets his fellow kin. The first of these monsters to look you up and down is just a hair smaller and thinner than Oak Root. "I am Nettle Branch." It says in a softer whispering like voice. "I am called Leaf Brow." Says the second in deep grunt. Leaf Brow is covered in thick large four pointed green leaves, and has only one glowing green eye. "I am Sage Trunk." Says the second largest of these beings. Sage Trunk has a much thicker base and a lighter coloration than the others and speaks with a hoarse echoing tone. You can feel so much magic emanating from these ancient beings; it is enough to make you feel like a tiny insect. "Well descendant of the Riven clan, will you come with us to the sacred grove?" Asks Oak Root.

If you wish to accompany the tree folk to the sacred grove turn to **264.**

If you would rather politely decline their offer and continue your mission turn to **163.**

192

You seize your moment to escape the arachnid duo assault, but as you turn away one of the slashing forearms grazes your leg. You shout in pain as the sharp edged weapon like arm cuts through your pants and tears through your flesh. You take **1d4** damage in the process of your escape. Despite the searing pain shooting through your wounded leg you run as fast and hard as you possibly can determined to escape the threat. The eight-legged horrors are right on your heels, desperate to catch the invader of their home. Just as your legs begin to weaken with exhaustion, and your heart and lungs feel like they are going to burst the two spiders abruptly stop in they're tracks and turn around and disappear. You stop, wondering why they had given up so easily? After you recover for a moment, you shrug off the bizarre behavior of the large spiders and continue to trek the tunnel. Soon you notice that the tunnel splits into two separate tunnels; there is one leading upward, and the other downward.

If you wish to trek the tunnel leading upward turn to **41.**

If you choose to take the tunnel leading downward turn to **211.**

193

You force your body to move faster, and your heart to beat harder. A second wind overcomes you and you feel a surge of vitality push you past your normal limits and soon you gain more and more ground from the bear. It roars and growls loudly at you frustration, then suddenly decides to give up its chase. You only stop when the beast is out of sight, (the use of this ability has cost you **2** magic points.) You rest and let your body gain its strength before deciding to continue. Night soon approaches; you must eat a meal or lose **4** health points. You decide not to fall asleep so quickly because of the noises and movement all around you; unsure of why there is more night activity than usual you wait to sleep until it quiets down a little. You awaken the following morning refreshed, you regain **3** health points. You begin to wonder how much longer you can take surviving and traveling this treacherous place, you pray that Allendrah is close and your journey will soon come to a close. The sun never breaks through the forest canopy today, and that sets a grim nervous mood for you as you travel.

The shadows of the trees dance around tauntingly, and the bird chirping soon comes to a dead silence. The tiny hairs on the back of your neck begin to stand up, and your heart pounds loudly in your chest as you approach a wall of briar patch that stretches as far as the eye can see and well over the trees. You stare at the strange overgrowth with confusion until you spot a single opening just ahead. Like the mouth of a dark cave it beckons to you, and you shrug your shoulders and walk over towards the opening. Realizing that this briar growth covers everything ahead this opening is the only way to progress ahead. Nervously you slowly enter the small mouth of the opening, careful not to get pricked by the thorns of the plant. The floor of what appears to be a tunnel is solid rock, dirt, and thick damp moss. It soon becomes dark like in a cave, (you must use stick and **1** magic point to create a spark to light your way unless you have a torch to spare.) After you have walked several more feet the tunnel forks into three different paths.

If you possess the ability of Fore-Sight and wish to use it turn to **45.**

If you do not possess this ability and would rather use Enhanced- Senses turn to **94.**

If you do not possess either of these abilities, but you have the Guardian ring turn to **109.**

If you do not possess the guardian ring and would like to take the tunnel leading left turn to **123.**

If you choose to the take the tunnel leading right turn to **161.**

If you would prefer to take the tunnel straight ahead turn to **205.**

194

You manage to get a lucky blow in, and knock Falco from his steed. He crashes to the ground cursing at you, you take this opportunity to keep going and Falco and his men have disappeared from view. You sigh in relief, and ride off into the night.

Turn to **174.**

195

With one last annoying clicking sound, the briar arachnid's body goes limp with death. You sigh over your victory in relief, but your glory is short lived though when you begin to hear more clicking noises approaching ahead. You are now aware that this labyrinth must be some sort of nest or hive for these bizarre creatures, you curse your unfortunate luck for stumbling into such a place but you do know that you must get out of here if you are find Allendrah. You must act quickly if you are to avoid these eight legged terrors that are quickly advancing through the tunnel towards your current position.

If you wish to run back down the tunnel to avoid these creatures turn to **257.**

If you possess the ability Spirit-Fire and wish to use it to attack these monsters then continue your trek through this tunnel turn to **303.**

If you do not possess this ability or would rather use the ability Elementalism turn to **334.**

If you do not possess either of these abilities or do not have the necessary amount of magic points, and would rather attack these creatures with your weapon turn to **17.**

A even closer look at the very ancient tombstones reveals that all three bear the numeral value of three on them, and also a short phrase on each in a language you almost do not recognize. You have very rarely seen the old written language of Riven clan mages; you realize this must have been an old Riven clan settlement and graveyard. The phrases on the gravestones read as follows:

Ones mind must remain clear.
Focus all energies onto one point.
Emotions must not cloud ones judgment.

You take a moment to ponder the three separate phrases and realize they are the three primary rules of the Riven clan students that are just learning the principles of magic. You wonder what the number three has to do with anything on the tombstones? You decide that the tombstones have no importance, or if they do you are not sure what the importance is? Intrigued by the crypt and what your ancestors may have left behind you walk over to the small building, it is covered in grave weeds, and dark green moss. Judging by the state the crypt is in you guess that the structure is well over a couple hundred years old. The entrance is blocked off by a large stone door with a strange type of locking mechanism that you are not familiar with, it is a dial with numerals all over it, it is complicated system of springs and gears but you realize that the door cannot open unless the dial is rotated to the correct numeral. There are two other dials that are stuck in place of a numeral, the sequence is as follows: the first is on the numeral **3,** and the second is on the numeral **6**. The third and last dial must be rotated on the correct numeral and you have numerals one to thirty available.

If you know the correct numeral that you must rotate the dial to turn to that section number.

If you wish to ignore the crypt and leave the graveyard turn to **112.**

If you possess the special ability Fore- sight and wish to use it turn to **256.**

If you do not possess this ability and cannot solve the mystery of the dial, and would rather explore the perimeter of the crypt for another way inside turn to **286.**

197

Before you can even react when you get the that something is terribly wrong, you hear the bowstring being pulled and you feel an arrow pierce into your shoulder. You take **1d6** damage. The bolt hit's the top of your shoulder and ricocheted into the darkness of the trees, you shout in pain as you turn to see your attacker. Your jaw is agape in horror as your eyes gaze upon a familiar figure appear from the shadows. The bandit leader has somehow managed to track you in the Azart Forest; he is more haggard looking than before from the tireless wandering through the woods. He sneers at you as he holds his long bow and another arrow in his dirty large hands. Those dark eyes pierce into your soul menacingly, and his scare makes him look far more fearsome than he did when you had first encountered this brute. "We meet again boy.., this time you will not get away." Hisses the large muscular bandit leader. You turn back and notice that the fae have vanished, though they are magical beings they are not fighters. "Traveling this treacherous forest has killed the rest of my men, after I have obtained that stone and gutted you boy I am going to enjoy burning this place down." Taunts the tall bandit as he steps closer towards you placing his arrow into his bow and taking aim.

If you possess a shield turn to **263.**

If you do not possess a shield you must roll the chance dice.

If you rolled 0-3 turn to **296.**

If you rolled a 4 or higher turn to **48.**

198

Your senses inform that these are the same men that invaded your home, and have somehow tracked you to this small village. You curse your misfortune; you know they are after the spirit stone. You watch as the bandit leader steps off his mount and walks in front of the gathered villagers. The bandit leader has a black thin goatee, a long scar down his left cheek, menacing dark eyes, and is very tall and muscular. You observe as he grabs one of the villagers by the throat, "We know that the person we are looking for has passed through here! Which way did he go?" The terrified villager is too frightened to respond, and is murdered in front of everyone as an example of how brutal he really is. The man is stabbed by a long black dagger carried by the bandit leader. "Very well we have other means of obtaining what we desire." The menacing mans deep voice echoes in the night as he signals his men to begin setting fire to the very inn in which you are in currently. You can hear the innocent villagers shouting in protest to the barbaric behavior of these bandits. You must act quickly if you are to escape unnoticed.

If you wish to run out the door and find safety turn to **247.**

Or if you would rather find an alternate means to escape turn to **349.**

199

You are soon in close proximity to something very strange, a large spider-like creature appears before. It is about three feet tall, dark green and black in coloration. It has a large single black eye in the center of its large head, and has two saw like serrated edged fore arms. For a brief moment the creature stares at you timidly as if to assess whether or not you are some kind of threat, and it begins to make loud clicking noises before it charges at you. It swings its sharp forearm at your midsection, you barely dodge the attack. With lightning fast reflexes you counter attack the strange half plant half spider creature, it moves far quicker than you had anticipated and avoids your attack. Despite the creatures speed you are prepared for its second assault.

Briar Arachnid
Attack. 10   **Health points. 13**
Armor class. 1   **Magic points. 0**

Hit: 1d4 +3

If you survive the combat turn to **195.**

200

You carefully using a stick dig a large pentagram in the ground between you and the tree folk, the massive being stares in fascination as you begin call upon the spirit world. At the cost of **4** magic points you chant in low whispers calling to any lost souls in the area to contact. Soon a ghostly apparition appears in the center of the pentagram, it is a middle aged man that is well built. He seems confused by his transparent state; some spirits do not even know that they are dead when they are channeled. The tree folk does appear to be alarmed by your ability, but shows no fear. "Why have you called upon my soul, all I want is rest." The ghost whispers as it stares at you with its white eyes. "To show this creature that I am who I am." You answer as you point at the tree folk. The ghost turns its attention to the tree before it, and it suddenly grows enraged. "It was this monster that has slain me!" It hisses as it stares at the tree folk with red eyes.

The tree folk growls loudly, "What sort of black magic is this? I killed this intruder when he was cutting down my trees.., and now you bring him back to my forest!" Loudly booms the giant's voice. "I needed lumber.., but now I will haunt you everyday until you are burnt into ashes." Howls the enraged spirit as it throws itself at the tree. The tree swats its large branches at the ghost, but due to its nature the attack does not even harm the spirit. "You are a foul mage of evil, be gone with you! Or you will suffer the same fate as this vile specter." Shouts the tree folk as it waves sparkling dust at the ghost, and banishes it from this realm of existence. You attempt to try to prove who you are, but the tree folk waves its branch like arms at you dismissively before lumbering away in a fit of rage.

Turn to **163.**

201

You are prepared for the assault of the two briar arachnids, they rush towards you quickly with a series of slashes that you dodge and avoid effortlessly. You cannot evade this fight; you are fighting for your life.

2 Briar Arachnids

Attack. 20	**Health points. 26**
Armor class. 2	**Magic points. 0**

Hit: 1d8+2

(Remember these creatures are weak to fire, incendiary potions and spirit-fire damage is doubled.)

If you survive the combat turn to **209.**

202

The tunnel that leads upward is much easier to trek, there is hardly any debris on the floor and a clear cool breeze pushes through the tunnel. Studying the architecture of the briar maze, you realize that the growth is natural but someone or something has done the tunneling. Who or what is a total mystery? You hope that you do not encounter the creator of the tunnels, several hours pass and the tunnel eventually becomes level but you cannot feel the fresh breeze any longer. It is not long before you can hear a loud scraping noise close by; the tunnel abruptly turns to the left. The scraping sound is just around the corner, your heart rate suddenly quickens as you wonder what is just around the corner?

If you wish to investigate the noise turn to **298.**
If you would rather go back the way you came turn to **338.**

203

You push your body to its limits and run without looking back, suddenly you hear the sound the arrow being fired. Without breaking your gate you press on, soon you can hear the whistling of the bolt flying in the air towards you. The arrow strikes the ground right behind you missing you entirely, with a sigh you notice you are out of his range and the bandit leader curses his shot. You are not in the clear yet though, now you hear shouting again but when you glance over your shoulder you see the bandit leader hopping onto a black stallions back. You must find a steed yourself; you will not be able to outrun bandits on horseback. Your eyes dart around your surroundings in desperation for a solution, and you notice a stable just ahead. There are several horses tied to the fence post, you hurriedly untie the nearest one and hop on its back. To your disappointment there is no saddle, but you are glad to see it has reins. With a quick jerk of the reins you shout, "Forward!" The horse does not move a muscle; you pinch the bridge of your nose in frustration. Your heart sinks in panic as the bandits are closing in quickly. You dig your heels into the horse's side, and without warning it breaks into full speed nearly sending you backwards on the ground. You grab on desperately and hold on for dear life.

Turn to **155.**

204

Suddenly one of the briar spiders appears in front of you, its large single black eye studying you carefully. You pause with your mouth agape, they are large then you had expected and more sinister looking also. It makes clicking noises as it stares at, then its bulbous abdomen pulsates and its mouth begins to move intensely like it is about spit something at you.

If you possess a shield and wish to use it turn to **265.**
If you do not possess a shield you must roll the chance dice.
If you rolled 0-3 turn to **7.**
If you rolled 4 or higher turn to **305.**

205

The tunnel directly ahead of you does not seem to be too difficult to travel; the ground however is covered in thick mud and forest debris. The temperature begins to rise, and sweat pours from your face. About thirty more minutes pass before you enter a strange chamber, it is circular with only one way out. But the most peculiar feature of this chamber is the walls are covered with large white pulsating sacs. You are not sure who or what has placed these here, but the are fused to the vines and briars of the wall by a strange webbing of some sort? Your curiosity overwhelms you as you raise your light source closer to the sacs; you can see the shapes moving around inside. Some kind of bug or bugs are inside, each about the size of your hand. You step back in surprise and disgust, and your presence has also stirred activity inside all of the sacs as they pulsate violently. You shudder in detest as the sacs start to rip open revealing dozens of palm sized spider like creatures, they are bright green with only one eye in the center of their heads. They make shrill squealing noises as they pour from their egg sacs and in a single coordinated wave rush towards you.

If you wish to flee from this brood chamber turn to **289.**

If you would rather stay and fight off these spiders turn to **321.**

206

The water is surprisingly cold, and the current is much stronger than it looks. It is difficult to remain standing, but you slowly walk deeper and deeper into the current. Suddenly you are pushed under the water, and you loose your footing. You can feel your leg and back being smashed into a large rock as the current continues to push you. Lose: **1** health point. You slowly regain your footing and slowly continue, but when the water level reaches your shoulders waves of cold water begin to smack you in the face. You must swim to the other side, and will be carried slightly downstream. Holding your breath you manage to fight the current for some time and reach the other side of the river, but your efforts have left you exhausted. You lose another health point. You quickly find the trail on the other side and continue to move along the path.

Turn to **4.**

207

Your only option is to slay the soldier briar arachnid in front of your only escape, or face certain death from an entire hive of spiders behind you. You do not have much time to fight this enemy off, if you do not kill your enemy quick enough you will be trampled to death by the spider horde.

Soldier Briar Arachnid

Attack. 14	**Health points. 18**
Armor class. 1	**Magic points. 0**

Hit: 1d6 + 3

(Remember that these creatures are weak to fire, incendiary potions and spirit-fire damage is doubled.)

If you win the combat in three rounds or less turn to **65.**

If you win the combat in four rounds or more turn to **136.**

208

Upon entering the smithy you behold a surprisingly spacious area, the armorer and weapons smithy are one in the same person. The owner is a large muscular man with a scorched apron, well build defined arms, he is wearing a steel cap, and has a broad nose with a long black mustache. He works the bellows intensely as he prepares to put the finishing touches on a sword. The smell of the metal heating is almost like sulfur, but you stand patiently as you watch the professional in his element. The large man suddenly notices your presence and halts his work to greet you. "Welcome stranger, I forge the best armaments in the land. Take your pick of anything that catches your fancy." Says the man in a deep voice as he points to his tables that are full of armor and weapons for your choosing.

1- <u>Dagger</u> - One-handed- Attack value- 4 (Damage: 1d4) cost: **2copper**

2 -<u>Rapier </u>- One-handed- Attack value -5 (Damage: 1d4+1) cost: **3copper**

3 -<u>Mace</u> -One-handed- Attack value -6 (Damage: 1d4+2) cost: **4 copper**

4 -<u>Axe</u> - One-handed -Attack value- 6 (Damage: 1d4+3) cost: **4 copper**

5- <u>War hammer </u>- One-handed -Attack value -7 (Damage: 1d6+1) cost: **5 copper**

6 -<u>Sword</u> -One-handed- Attack value -8 (Damage: 1d6+2) cost: **6 copper**

7 -<u>Staff</u> -Two-handed - Attack value- 7 (Damage: 1d6) (Adds one extra point of damage to spirit- fire) cost: **4 copper**

8 -<u>Large Axe</u> -Two-handed -Attack value -9 (Damage: 1d6+ 4) cost: **8 copper**

9- <u>Broadsword </u>-Two- handed - Attack value-10 (Damage: 1d8+3) cost: **10 copper**

0 -Spear -Two-handed -Attack value-11 (Damage: 1d8+4) cost: **14 copper**

*- Bow -Two-handed - Attack value- 8 (Damage: 1d8) cost: **8copper**

*- Cross-Bow - Two-handed -Attack value-12 (Damage: 1d8+4) cost: **15 copper**

*- Pole-Axe -Two-handed- Attack value -13 (Damage: 1d10+3) cost: **20 copper**

*-Quiver containing: 10 Arrows or bolts - **Cost: 1 Copper**

Armor

1 - Wooden shield - armor class-1- reduces combat damage by 1 point. Cost: **5 copper**

2 - Buckler -armor class -1- reduces combat damage by 2 points. Cost: **10 copper**

3 - Large shield -armor class-2- reduces combat damage by 2 points. Cost: **20 copper**

4 -Tower shield - armor class-2- reduces combat damage by 3 points. Cost: **30 copper**

5- Skullcap - armor class-1. Cost: **4 copper**

6- Studded leather vest - armor class-1. Cost: **6 copper**

(After you have finished purchasing any equipment do not forget to adjust your character sheet properly, Also you may sell any equipment you have at half the price rounded down to the smith.) You decide to ask the armorer about the Azart Forest before he can get back to his work but he tells you he does not know how to reach that awful cursed place.

If you wish to obtain information at the tavern turn to **58.**

Or if you would rather try to get information from the herbalist shop turn to **102.**

209

The tunnel remains a daunting task to traverse, time does not seem quick enough here. You cannot stand the smell, look, or feel of this place any longer. You do not want to think about how many networks of tunnels could have been created by these foul monsters, the tunnels could be endless. You are very exhausted and feel drained from your traveling; you pause to rest for a moment. When you feel more refreshed and able to continue your quest you recover **2** health points, and **1** magic point. After another hour of slowly working your way through the sewer like tunnel, it begins to slope upward slightly onto a more even level ground where the mud has hardened. You are slightly relieved that you are not going to trek through more sticky thick mud.

Turn to **41.**

210

Using your free hand you extend your palm at the nearest hulking green troll, it does not appear to alarmed by your gesture. "Come here supper!" Growls the large troll as it reaches for you. With the expense of **1** magic point you fire a single jet of searing white fire at the troll, it wails in torment as it covered in flames. The other troll shouts in surprise as it watches its comrade trying to put out the flames, "Ock mad now! I will smash this man thing." The unharmed troll shouts as it holds a wooden club in one hand and charges at you. (Due to being upside down you must deduct **2** from your attack. Also if you have a shield it cannot be used for this combat since you dropped it from being snared in the trap.)

Troll

Attack. 14   **Health points. 26**
Armor class. 1   **Magic points. 0**

Hit: 1d8 +1

Trolls are weak to spirit-fire; damage done with this spell in combat is doubled. If you survive the combat you manage to free yourself from the trap and land on the ground.

Turn to **23.**

211

The tunnel leading downward begins to make you very nervous, the air is so humid and warm that you find it difficult to breath properly. You cough hoarsely, but force yourself to continue. Soon you are in almost knee deep sticky warm mud, having to make quick movements will prove to be a hindering challenge. You pray that you are not going to be set upon by any briar arachnids, but just as your nerves begin to calm slightly you notice several briar arachnids heading straight for you. You quickly turn in hopes to back track and escape through the other tunnel, but you see a large horde of spiders pouring in the way you came. There is no escaping your sealed fate, you manage to kill scores of these fearsome predators but you are eventually overwhelmed by their numbers and you are torn to shreds.

Your life and quest end here gruesomely.

212

You quickly remove a antidote from your backpack, and remove the cork then drink the bitter contents of the brew. Almost immediately the effects of the poison subside, you feel instant relief from the gas as it begins to engulf you more. The antidote will only work for a little while longer; you have the opportunity to rush past the cloud without it affecting you. Holding your breath you run to the end of the mushroom ring field to safety. As soon as you are at a reasonable distance the mushroom caps stop shaking and producing the toxic sleeping gas.

Turn to **348.**

213

Your only option is to fight this adversary before the spider host behind you catches up to you; you could never win against such overwhelming odds. With your weapon ready, you attack the large spider without slowing your pace. The black intimidating arachnid welcomes your attack, and with a loud hissing cry you are swept into combat.

Soldier Briar Arachnid

Attack. 14   **Health points. 18**

Armor class. 1   **Magic points. 0**

Hit: 1d6 +3

(These creatures are weak to fire, incendiary potions and spirit-fire damage is doubled.)

If you win the combat in three rounds or less turn to **65.**

If you win the combat in three rounds or more turn to **136.**

214

You look around your surroundings and you see a very large bear nearby, it is about seven feet tall with long grizzled dark brown hear and has very large sharp teeth. It immediately locks eyes with you; its dark black eyes intimidate you and leave you frozen where you stand. The large beast stands up on its hind feet and roars again very loudly, before charging right at you.

If you wish to run turn to **295.**

If you possess Spirit-Fire and wish to use it turn to **326.**

If you would prefer to stand your ground and fight the bear turn to **30.**

215

You cautiously enter the burning structure, immediately the thick black smoke chokes your airway and you cough violently but you still push yourself on. Lose **1** Health point due to inability to breath. The smoke also blinds you and makes your eyes water and burn intensely as you follow the sound of your father's pleas. Suddenly you hear cracking as the roofing of the home begins to fall above you. (You must roll the chance dice.)

If you rolled 0-4 turn to **64.**
If you rolled 5 or higher turn to **111.**

216

As you whisper the enchantment of illusion, you wince as you brace yourself for your tragic death. The tidal wave of large bugs are soon upon you, but to your surprise the stone casts a milky white glow just as you have seen in when your mentor first had shown you the rock. The blinding white light encircles you protectively as the spiders surround you, the first wave of spiders are blinded by the intensity of the light, but the hundreds of others behind them continue their charge. You prepare yourself for the impact of such numbers descending upon you, but to your surprise the spiders pass through you as if you were never there in the first place. To your shock you are transparent, barely visible. You are like a spirit; you are still there but stuck in between this reality and another.

The spiders relentlessly attack you, but are unable to harm you at all. Smiling in relief you do not even bother to avoid further attack from these beings, you take your weapon and strike at one of the briar arachnids. Despite being an apparition you are able to inflict damage, while you are unable to receive it. You take this opportunity to let yourself sink into a berserk like state, and attack every single briar arachnid that dares cross your weapons path. After a long endless moment of brutal combat you manage to slay many, and when the survivors realize that this is a fight they cannot win they shriek in frustration and flee. After the surviving spiders are out of sight, you relax and take a deep breath. The bright light of the spirit stone dims slightly and you become fully corporeal again, the stones magic has worn off. You thank the spirit of your mentor for once again guiding you through a fatal moment, you feel completely re-energized and refreshed. (Restore all lost health points and magic points to their original totals.) Just as you prepare to continue your quest something in the distance catches your eyes.

Turn to **241.**

217

You tread westward without the ease of a trail, since there is a peculiar enchantment cast over the forest basic navigation skills will not work. You will only have your abilities and instincts to guide you and you have gone too far to fail now. You notice that you cannot travel as quickly because off all the rocks and sudden steep levels of the forest floor, but you continue west anyway. After the rain finally ends, do you pause to dry your clothes and make yourself more comfortable. Right before you grab your backpack to continue, a strange aroma fills your nostrils and grabs your curiosity. You can faintly smell something being cooked just ahead, you wonder if you are the only traveler here or if someone else has made a campsite and is now cooking meat. The smell is delicious and inviting, but you do not know who or what is preparing the main course.

If you wish to investigate the location of the smell turn to **85.**

If you would rather ignore the odor and continue your course turn to **318.**

218

You dash past the two spiders in front of you and run down the tunnel leading downward, the sound of clicking is right on your heels as you force your body to move. The terrain down this tunnel quickly becomes more and more difficult to run in, the mud becomes stickier and thicker slowing you down tremendously. Soon you are knee deep in water mud, you glance over your shoulder just to see one of the spider leaping into the air. Using your weapon you sweat the creature away, it shrieks in pain and lands in the mud. Two more appear right behind it and before you know it you have been slashed in your midsection , the wound is deep. Next you feel an intense burning sensation throughout your back, you peel away your clothes to notice a green acidic like fluid all over it. You attempt to put up a good fight, but every attack you fend off, you are struck from another angle by your attackers slashing fore arms until you are too weak to fight back.

Your life and quest end here.

219

Exerting **2** magic points you focus your minds eye on the current event that is taking place with the moving of the forest, and your abilities warn you that the ruby that was removed from the statue plays a magical element with a spell that allows the path to Allendrah to be sought. Removing the rare sparkling gem has triggered the spell to turn off, you wonder if placing the gem back inside the owl statue will allow the spell to work again?

If you wish to return the gem to the owl statue turn to **260.**

If you would rather keep the valuable gem and walk in the direction that the arrow was pointing turn to **312.**

220

Sensing your aggression the wolf charges at you with its glistening teeth bared hungry for your flesh. You cannot evade this combat, this fight is to the death.

Large wolf

Attack. 10   **Health points. 14**
Armor class. 1   **Magic points. 0**

Hit : 1d6 +1

If you survive the combat turn to **316.**

221

Traveling in the eastern direction is proving very difficult, even after the rainfall has finally stopped there are many large mud pools to trek through. After long exhausting walks and wading through mud holes waist deep you lose your boots, and are unable to recover them. (Subtract **1** point from your armor class.) Hours slowly pass and you make little progress on the unstable terrain, and you are even beginning to wonder if you are even heading in the right direction. You start to think that you are going in circles, everything looks the same and you even start to find some of your foot prints. You attempt to back track them a little in hopes of leading you back to where the trail ended, but some of your tracks look like they are coming from every other direction making it impossible to discern new tracks from old. One could go mad in this forest after days of circling the same area, paranoia and fear start to fill your mind as you dread getting lost in here forever. You must roll the chance dice.

If you rolled 0-4 turn to **268.**
If you rolled 5 or higher turn to **13.**

222

You only manage to take a few steps past the strange creatures, when one of them turns abruptly in your direction.

It clicks loudly to its comrade and slowly begins to approach your position. You bite your lips in frustration as you stand motionless as the eight legged horror creeps closer, the second spider now also appears curious and slowly falls in behind the first spider. You curse your luck when you notice that your invisibility cloak is wearing off, the two spiders screech in surprise as you materialize in front of them. You step back in alarm as they launch an attack upon you.

2 Briar Arachnids

Attack. 20   **Health points. 26**
Armor class. 2   **Magic points. 0**

Hit : 1d8 +3

If you survive the combat turn to **314.**

223

You dash out in front of the two closest bandits and with the expense of **1** magic point you release a searing white jet of flames from your hand, both the bandits are engulfed in flames and scream in agony. The surrounding villagers notice your attack and with renewed enthusiasm grab whatever they can use as a weapon and charge at the remaining bandits. As you lead the way through the fray and chaos, a lone bandit appears in front of you with his weapon drawn and a gleeful smile on his dirty face. You must fight this bandit to the death.

Bandit

Attack. 13   **Health points. 16**

Armor class. 2   **Magic points. 0**

Hit : 1d6 +1

After you land the final blow on the enemy, he crashes to the ground dead. There is no time to loot the body, you must escape and you run. After you tear around the next corner of a building you hear shouting in the distance, and two more bandits spring out in front of you.

Turn to **6.**

224

You release the bolt, but to your dismay the creature avoids the attack completely and leaps onto you. You both crash onto the ground struggling to win the fight, you feel a sharp stinging pain in your side. One of the slashing arms of the spider has cut your side, you wince at the sight of your own blood. You lose **2** health points. The creature clicks and hisses at you as you strike at it with your weapon, you manage to land an attack on its eye. The arachnid squeals in pain, you have successfully damaged its eye. Killing the large spider with ease, you take full of advantage of its blindness. After the creature writhes on the floor and suddenly dies, you make haste to continue along the tunnel. It soon forks, with one tunnel leading upward and the other downward.

If you wish to take the tunnel leading upward turn to **41.**

If you choose to take the tunnel leading downward turn to **211.**

225

You land the finishing blow on the last wolf, and it goes crashing to the ground dead. This epic struggle for your life has taken its toll and you are exhausted, and your clothing is terribly tattered and filthy. You look and feel like a ragged vagrant beggar that has been living off the street for months, you slowly limp past the dead wolf corpses and try to leave the area before more of they 're kind appear. You find yourself stumbling and unable to walk, you are too weak to continue on. Landed head first on the forest floor, you succumb to a very deep and much needed slumber. When you awaken you are surprised to find yourself in the state you are in, it is also the middle of the day. Feeling refreshed you yawn loudly, and pat the dirt from your tattered clothing. Your rest has recovered **4** health points and **2** magic points. After you have your bearings straightened out, you realize that you are starving. You must eat one meal or lose **4** health points. After your meal, you continue your long trek through the Azart Forest.

Turn to **3.**

226

With a brilliant display of skill with your abilities you release a single jet of searing hot white flames onto one of your

attackers. The arachnid hisses as it attempts to put the flames out that cover its burning body, the use of this ability has cost you **1** magic point. Your attack on the first spider does not seem to deter the second from attacking, it leaps into the air at you. You must roll the chance dice.

If you rolled 0-3 turn to **319**.
If you rolled 4 or higher turn to **26**.

227

You pause while the bandits circle the nearby area looking for anything that had the horses on nerve. Your patience pays off, while their attention is in the opposing direction that you are in you have the opportunity to slip right past them unnoticed. You stick to the shadows and quietly sneak out of your home village, and then when the bandits are out of sight you make a quick dash for the Lorna grasslands.

Turn to **36**.

228

At the cost of **1** magic point you aim your open hand up over your head and release a hissing jet of white spirit-fire into the chamber of the crypt, the glimmer of the fiery white light brightens the room and fills it with a warmth that is comforting and soothing. Immediately after the fire is extinguished a hidden door of stone in the floor between the two sarcophagi opens up reveal a new chamber for you. You glance down into the next chamber, there is a set of stairs for you to follow into the next room. You also notice that there is light source down inside the second chamber.

If you wish to explore the next room of this ancient crypt turn to **346.**

If you would rather leave the crypt and continue your quest to find Allendrah turn to **121.**

229

You fire your bolt, but to your unfortunate luck the bolt barely misses its target. The large black spider clicks and hisses at you aggressively before it leaps at you with its slashing arms, you step back avoiding the lethal attack and have your other weapon ready to defend yourself. You must fight this creature to the death.

Soldier Briar Arachnid

Attack. 13	**Health points. 18**
Armor class. 1	**Magic points. 0**

Hit: 1d6 +3

(Remember that these creatures are weak to fire, incendiary potions and spirit-fire damage is doubled.)

If you survive the combat turn to **327.**

230

You approach the large walking tree very cautiously, it seems oblivious to your presence. The large tree stands about thirty feet tall, has large thick dark brown and gray bark covering its entire body. Its roots appear to be two large flat feet like structures that allow its movement, it has deep set glowing green eyes, a very wide uneven mouth, and long stringy white and light green moss growing all over its large face. The lumbering creature is spreading some sort dirt all over the trail and nearby plant life, and mumbling to itself as it continues its labors. You have never seen such a sight before and wonder what type of monster this is? The large tree monster suddenly stops what it is doing and faces you with its glowing green eyes, "What fleshy creature might thou be in thy sanctuary? Answer me quickly, or suffer my wrath pale skin!" The tree barks with a low rumbling voice that shakes the entire forest.

If you wish to answer the strange giant and reveal the details of who you are and your mission turn to **68.**

Or if you would rather lie, and not divulge the details of your quest turn to **176.**

231

Your first shot misses, but you quickly reload and aim again. Your second shot sails true to its target and fells one of the spiders, the arrow has pierced its head and brain. The second spider leaps into the air and slams its body into yours, your bow/crossbow is knocked from your arms. You quickly recover from the jarring attack, and the briar arachnid is attacking you with its forearms. You must fight this creature unarmed for the first round of combat.

Soldier Briar Arachnid

Attack. 13	**Health points. 18**
Armor class. 1	**Magic points. 0**

Hit : 1d6 +3

(Remember these creatures are weak to fire, incendiary potions and spirit-fire damage is doubled.)

After you have slain the spider, you recover your bow/crossbow. (Remember to mark off the use of **2** arrows from your quiver on your character sheet.) You make haste along the gruesome tunnel, it winds and turns almost endlessly but you soon arrive at a fork in the tunnel. One tunnel leads upward and the other leads downward.

If you wish to take the tunnel leading upward turn to **41.**

If you would rather take the tunnel leading downward turn to **211.**

232

With your weapon ready the large bear tears over towards you snarling aggressively, you cannot evade this fight it is to the death.

Large Bear

Attack. 18	**Health points. 30**

Armor class. 3   **Magic points. 0**

Hit : 1d6 +5

If you survive turn to **5.**

233

Exerting **3** magic points you slip into everyone's blind spot unnoticed. You do not have much time to escape before your ruse wears off, so quickly you make your way towards the door. Right when you are about to open the large wooden door, it opens quickly. You freeze in your steps and alarm, in the door frame is perhaps the most sinister looking off all the bandits. The man is very tall, has a long scar down his left cheek, burning eyes, and is very muscular. His lock with yours, and you can only stare back not sure if he can see past your illusion. The man walks inside the bar, his thick leather boots stomping on the hardwood floor loudly. You sigh relieved that you were not seen and you slip through the door before it shuts tightly again. You notice that the spell is wearing off and you are becoming visible again, you must act quickly and leave this village.

Turn to **31.**

234

Your bolt sails true and accurately as it impales the creature's eye, the force from your shot knocks it back as it leaps towards you. With a shrill squeal the spider like monster twitches slightly before going limp with death, you sigh at your dead on shot that neutralized that threat. You victory is short lived however when you begin to hear more clicking noises all around you. There is a lot of noise just ahead of you, and notice from the shadows from your only light source that there must be at least three more of these fearsome spider like creatures rapidly approaching.

If you wish to turn back and find another tunnel to traverse turn to **11.**

If you would rather remain where you are and face these creatures with your bow or crossbow turn to **283.**

235

The last briar arachnid squeals as you strike it in the eye, and like a pus joule that is being squeezed it bursts and green fluid splashes all over. You sigh with relief, you have never seen such ferocity in bugs before. You decide it is best to keep moving before more appear, the tunnel winds in many directions and you begin to notice that the farther you manage to get the easier it is to travel along this tunnel. The ground is no longer muddy and sticky, it is not as humid and uncomfortable either. Sunlight pokes through the roof of the tunnel, you are about to take a rest when you suddenly more loud clicking behind you. Forcing your legs to carry you as swiftly as possible, you are determined to reach the end of this infernal place. You glance back over your shoulder and notice a horde of these spiders clicking and screeching loudly, there are too many to count. You do however have a lot of ground on these monsters, and just as you are certain that you will keep them at bay you notice one of them blocking your path just ahead, but this one is different. This lone briar spider is slightly larger in size, and is a solid black color and its forearms are much larger in proportion to its other counterparts. It hisses loudly, then spit's a stream of green fluid at you. You effortlessly sidestep the attack slowing down, and then the large spider charges at you. You must fight this creature to continue your escape through this tunnel.

Soldier Briar Arachnid

Attack. 14   **Health points. 18**
Armor class. 1   **Magic points. 0**

Hit: 1d6 + 3

(Remember that these creatures are weak to fire, incendiary potions and spirit-fire damage is doubled.)

If you win the combat in three rounds or less turn to **65.**

If you win the combat in four rounds or more turn to **136.**

236

Unable to decide which direction you should take, you without even thinking about it trek off in the unknown ahead of you. Full of uncertainty and confusion you only hope that blind luck will get you to your destination alive. The rain continues to fall on you while you move through thick mud holes nearly waist deep, and you lose your boots suddenly and are unable to locate them. (Subtract **1** point from your armor class.) The hours pass you by very slowly and you are not making good progress, you begin to notice foot prints in the distance in the wet mud. Upon your investigating, you discover they are in fact your own foot prints. You have been going in circles, but for long is uncertain. You shout your frustration, and attempt to back track a ways in hopes of find the spot where the trail ended. To your dismay and unfortunate luck your tracks lead in so many different directions that you are unable to properly navigate this wilderness. You must roll the chance dice.

If you rolled 0-4 turn to **268.**
If you rolled 5 or higher turn to **13.**

237

You slowly and cautiously trek the left path, hours fly by without incident. You begin to wonder if you will arrive in the Azart Forest before nightfall, but as your mind wanders on the uncertain future something catches your eyes in the distance. You aren't sure of what you had just seen in that brief moment, but it sends shivers down your spine. Again something movers in the distances between some bushes just ahead, but you cannot make out the source of the movement. Your horse suddenly becomes very nervous and tries to turn around, but you keep your mount on course against its wishes. Suddenly you hear what you think is the twang of a bowstring, and suddenly you feel an arrow slam into your chest. In shock you try to breath and make an escape but you are immediately pulled off your horse by two scrawny hood covered men, and they smash your head open with a rock and rob you, and leave you die in the middle of the dirt path.

Your life and quest end here.

238

The left tunnel leads upwards a little, a cool soothing breeze flows freely through this tunnel and dries the sweat from your brow as you cautious press onward. You do notice that even though the briar and vine growth is natural, something had to have created these tunnels. But who or what? You pray that you will not find out, you must find a way to the other side of this maze is you are to reach Allendrah. You notice that for the first time the tunnel makes an abrupt right turn, and as you approach the corner you begin to hear something shuffling towards you. You freeze in your steps and hold your breath, you had hoped that you were alone but something is close by.

If you wish to investigate what is moving around the corner turn to **292.**

If you would rather turn back the way you came and take another tunnel turn to **338.**

239

You close your eyes and glimpse into the past, present, and future briefly. With the cost of **2** magic points you see images of a time not so long ago when fae first arrived in the Azart

Forest, You can see strange beings announcing the name of the ferry queen. Suddenly a name is imprinted deeply in your minds eye. The secret name of the ferry queen is now apparent to you.

Continue, by turning to **43.**

240

You quickly discover that the blaze is the result of an attack, by who and what are unknown to you? As you approach the first building that was set ablaze you do not notice anyone of your village around the flames, but you do notice many boot prints and hoof prints. The attackers were on horse back, and of the looks of it you identify seven steeds and at least ten others that were not on horseback. You must be careful not to be detected by the attackers, for there are too many of them for you to fight. Suddenly your thoughts are on your family, and with break neck speed you charge for your farmhouse.

Turn to **300.**

241

At first you think that your eyes have deceived you when you notice a cloud of twinkling dust approaching you, rubbing your eyes with disbelief you focus closer on the strange sight as it closes in. Unsure if you are in any danger you attempt to channel more energy into the spirit stone, but nothing happens as the soft milky white light warms you. The strange cloud of rainbow colored dust appears to have strange insect like beings flying inside of it, you squint as you try to see what you are looking at more closely. Suddenly you are enveloped inside the cloud of magical glamour, the small beings that are floating freely inside have bug like wings and the appearance of tiny humans. At once it dawns on you what you are gazing upon, the legendary fae. They must have sensed the energy of the spirit stone when it was activated, they are drawn to the aura of the magical stone that you bear tightly in your hands. The small sprites flicker and giggle around you delightfully, you must be on guard though they are the escorts to Allenedrah they do not know who you are or what your mission is. Their interest is the stone, and you must somehow arrange for these ferries to take you to your destination?

If you have visited the Sacred Grove earlier in your adventure turn to **324.**

If you have never visited such a place before turn to **37.**

242

You hold your breath and clench your weapon tightly as the troll duo approaches, you can hear their breathing as they close in. One of the tall lumbering oaf's appears right next to you, nearly jumping in alarm you manage to hold your position without being noticed. The second troll however spots you and shouts to his comrade, and that is when you spring into action.

If you wish to flee turn to **308.**
If you wish to stand your ground and fight turn to **56.**

243

You instinctively step to the side and duck slightly, barely in enough time to avoid being struck by the arrow that whistles past your ears. You turn around in surprise to see a familiar figure appear from the shadows of the forest, it is the bandit leader that you have encountered before your entry into the Azart Forest. He has somehow managed to follow you this far into this dangerous forest? "We meet again boy!" Hisses the deep voice of the tall muscular haggard looking bandit with the long scar down his left cheek. "This time you will not escape my wrath." He adds full of hate in his tone. You turn around and notice that Oona and her escorts have vanished. Though they are magical guardians of the forest, they are not fighters. "This awful place has killed all of my men, and almost myself several times but not even a dark forest will stop me boy." Taunts the evil man as he steps closer loading another bolt in his long bow and aiming it right at your chest.

If you possess a shield turn to **263.**
If you do not possess a shield you must roll the chance dice.
If you rolled 0-2 turn to **296.**
If you rolled a 3 or higher turn to **48.**

244

Your finely attuned senses alert you to the presence of at three predators hunting you, your guess is it is wolf. You can sense one right in front of you, and the other two scouting the surrounding area keeping a close eye on you. Your intuition tells you that the first wolf will attempt to get you to run towards the other two wolves so that you will be overwhelmed and unable to escape. You must do something, these predators are not going to let you out of their sight. Without warning the first wolf leaps in front of you, it has long grizzly gray and brown hair, piercing yellow eyes, and is far larger than you had anticipated. It growls loudly at you with its glistening white teeth bared.

If you wish to stand your ground and fight this lone wolf turn to **220.**

If you choose to flee instead turn to **182.**

245

Immediately you have fired your first shot, it sails into the first spider that is about to strike killing it instantly. Your attack has not deterred the attack from the next spider as it approaches, and you quickly load another shot and prepare to fire. You must roll the chance dice.

If you rolled 0-3 turn to **32.**

If you rolled a 4 or higher turn to **96.**

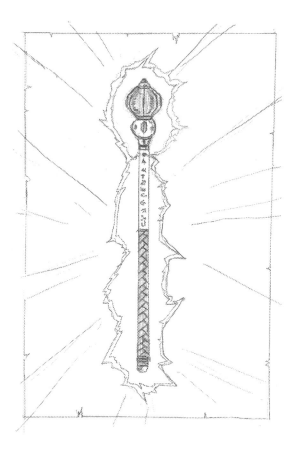

246

You carefully walk over to the new chamber, it is a Simicircular room that is extremely tiny and sitting in the center of a pedestal is a golden scepter. You can feel the warmth of the magic of this weapon all around you, it is enchanted with powerful spells that can aid you in your quest. A closer inspection of the scepter reveals a solid handle with riven symbols all over it, and many small jewels crafted into the weapon. The second your hands touch the mystical tool, a golden aura bathes you. (If you wish to keep this weapon mark it as the **Mystical Scepter,** if it is not equipped you must carry it as a backpack item. Listed below are the magical properties of this legendary weapon that was once used by Ulzar and Elaine the two most legendary magi of your order.)

Mystical Scepter
One-handed weapon Attack. **10**
Damage: 1d4 +6
-Deals double damage to the undead.
- Restores two extra health point when casting curing.
-Adds two extra damage to spirit-fire.(In combat only.)

After you have removed the mace from its pedestal, you hear a click and then the stairs suddenly retract from where they had early disappeared to and the door to the first floor opens also allowing you to leave the crypt.

Turn to **121.**

247

You run outside the door of the Inn, but to your misfortune there are several bandits' right outside. They immediately notice you, and with weapons drawn they advance. You curse your foolish decision, your mentor would be very disappointed with your hastiness.

If you wish to run back inside and find another way to escape turn to **349.**

Or if you would rather attempt to outrun the bandits turn to **6.**

248

You bite your upper lip nervously as you quickly recite the dark art litany, and channel that energy into the lifeless rock of the spirit stone. The spider horde is almost upon, and just as you think that you have failed your mission the stone awakens with a fury of bright white light. Your jaw is agape as you witness the re-awakening of the almighty vessel of all magic, the arachnid's pause cowering before the blinding surge of light and awesome power. You feel a dark force approaching, shadows as black as night dance around you and the spider army before you. You shiver as a cold chill runs through your whole body, never before have you felt such a power before. You wonder if you are in control of this unpredictable power? And your doubts are soon washed away as the light of the spirit stone dims slightly and bones begin to appear out of the ground suddenly, they all vary in shape and size as they circle you. You welcome the spells effects as the bones protectively form a impenetrable barrier around you just as the stalled spider force regains their courage to continue their attack. The spiders cover you and attack ferociously, but they are unable to get through the bone barrier that protects you from all of their attacks. Without warning the barrier suddenly explodes with such force that the arachnid force is splintered, the shards of sharp bone pierce your enemies and kill many. The few spiders that do manage to survive the attack hiss at you before fleeing, you sigh with relief. (Restore all lost health points and magic points to their original totals.) After a much needed relaxing moment, you decide to continue your search for Allendrah but something new has caught your attention.

Turn to **241.**

249

Despite the desperation of the current circumstance you calmly chant to the void of the elemental realm for assistance, the two menacing trolls appear to not notice you in your serene trance. "I get first taste Ock!" Growls one of the beasts as he reaches for you, the other swats his arm away violently and roars loudly with green foam frothing from its large crooked mouth. "It was my trap that caught our supper, I get first taste!" The two monsters stare at each other angrily, you smile at this opportunity that will bye you time for the elementals aid you. They begin to exchange blows with one another, mostly shoving and solid smacks upside the head. You watch as they wrestle to determine the pecking order of their hierarchy, you hope that elemental assistance comes soon. Suddenly the wind begins to pick up, and a funnel shaped torrent of wind magic appears before you. You recognize the gale as a wind elemental, and sensing your need for assistance the growing tornado descends upon the bickering troll duo. They are immediately carried off the ground and slammed against one another repeatedly until they are both unconscious and motionless on the ground. The cost for elemental aid has cost you **2** magic points. You waste no time to free yourself and flee the scene as quickly as possible.

Turn to **42.**

250

Suddenly one of the spiders appears behind you, it immediately notices you and screeches loudly to its other two comrades. You curse your unfortunate luck when all three spider spring into action, the large one in front of you arch's its body back slightly and its abdomen pulsates and suddenly it spit's a stream of green fluid at you.

If you possess a shield and wish to use it turn to **309.**
If you do not possess a shield you must roll the chance dice.
If you rolled 0-3 turn to **29.**
if you rolled a 4 or higher turn to **133.**

251

The last of the wolf trio finally falls to the ground dead, you sigh with relief and take a moment to compose yourself. (You may take enough wolf meat for up to 5 meals if you choose.) You continue your daunting trek onward through the forest, it isn't until a couple of incident free hours pass before something catches your eye. Beside the moss overgrown trail are clumps of different herbs growing, as well as a berry bush next to the trail on the opposite side.

You recognize the berry bush as a merry berry bush, the tiny red round bulb like berries are a delicacy and used for pies all over western and central Lamara. (You may pick enough merry berries for up to 2 meals.)

If you possess the special ability of Herbalism and wish to use it turn to **2.**

If you do not or wish to resume your mission turn to **60.**

252

Expending **1** magic point you aim your open palm at the charging threat is bounding towards you, a screaming jet of white flames covers the bandit leader. He screams in pain, but the injury does not stop him from slamming his flaming body into yours. The flames from your own attack now cover you, you desperately attempt to put the fire out and fight Falco at the same time, but you are quickly losing the battle. Soon your spirit is looking upon your charred body, as Falco removes the Spirit stone and gives a triumphant yell of victory. The world of Lamara is now forever covered in the shadowy embrace of evil forever.

Your life and quest end here.

253

The crypt is very old, the stone walls are worn down and covered in grave weeds and dark green moss. Judging by the condition of the place you figure that this old graveyard must be well over a couple hundred years old. You notice that the entrance is blocked by a very large stone door with a complicated locking mechanism that you have never seen the likes of before. There are three dials, two of which are locked into place on a numeral. Numerals you recognize as Riven Clan symbols, to your surprise you realize that this is an old Riven clan graveyard. You are amazed by your ancestor's ingenuity, You have not seen architecture like this in your own home. The two dials that are locked into a position land on the numbers **3**, and **6**. The last dial is free to rotate from the numerals one through thirty, you must figure out what numeral to rotate the dial to unlock the crypt door.

If you know the correct numeral that you must rotate the dial to turn to that section number.

If you wish to ignore the crypt and leave the graveyard turn to **112.**

If you possess the special ability Fore- sight and wish to use it turn to **256.**

If you do not possess this ability and cannot solve the mystery of the dial, and would rather explore the perimeter of the crypt for another way inside turn to **286.**

254

You use all of energy and channel into the mighty spirit stone, you can feel a surge of righteous power become a concentrated beam of power that is blasted directly at Falco. The moment the power hits him, he stops and laughs. "You expect a rock to defeat me boy!" Suddenly you observe the evil shadowy aura grow to immense proportions and begin to fight off the pure energy that you have sent into the bandit leader. You attempt to fight off the evil power, but it is putting up a good fight. You are not about to give up you are going to use however much power it will take to defeat this evil. You must roll the chance dice.

If you rolled 0-2 turn to **101.**
If you rolled a 3 or higher turn to **156.**

255

With the expense of **3** magic points, you close your eyes and focus your powers on the enchantment. Within moments you are completely invisible and begin to walk right past the guards, even though the bandits do not notice your presence the horses both are starring right at you watching you advance past them. You assume that they can either sense you or smell you, but that does not tip the bandits off that there is someone right in front of them. Soon you are well ahead of the bandits before the spell wares off and you are visible, then you slink away for the Lorna grasslands.

Turn to **36.**

256

After exerting **2** magic points and focusing on the dial in front of you and the clues that you have obtained thus far, your intuition reminds you that Riven Clan rules and guidelines are based on the primary number and rule of three's. Everything about the field of magic and its properties are based on multiples of three, the numbers that the first two dials are locked onto are the clues. The numbers **3**, **6** are multiples of three. So the next number in the sequence and the key to opening this mechanism is going to be a multiple of three.

If you have solved the mystery of the puzzle turn to the section number.

If you are unable to figure out the next number of the sequence turn to **286.**

257

You turn around and run in the opposite direction that the noises are coming from, the clicks soon turn into loud screeching noises that ring your ears. They know there is an intruder, you figure that they discovered they're slain kin and are now on the hunt for you. You manage to backtrack to a fork in the tunnels this time you take the tunnel leading downward, the floor is covered in a layer of water and sticky warm mud. You find it difficult to move quickly, and the humidity is making you sweat profusely. The tunnel leads into a large chamber that has strange white pulsating sac's stuck to the walls, unsure of what these things are you avoid contact with them. As you turn for the exit of the strange chamber, you begin to hear strange noises coming from the sacs. You turn in horror to discover that the sacs are holding the young of these spider creatures, each about the size of your hand. There is a flood of this terrifying brood, and they are attracted to the light that you are giving off with your torch. You must fight these younglings so that you are not hindered in your progress.

Briar Arachnid Brood

Attack. 10   **Health points. 20**
Armor class. 3   **Magic points. 0**

Hit: 1d4

If you survive the combat turn to **14.**

258

You get close enough to study the large unusual cluster of mushrooms before you, you are not familiar with this type of fungus but you can tell by the resin that the caps are secreting that it might be some type of poison. You assume that the mushrooms are not safe to make contact with, and the foul smell coming from the mushrooms is also an indicator that it is a highly toxic breed.

If you wish to back track the trail and find a alternate route to travel through the forest turn to **28.**
Or if you wish to ignore your knowledge of basic herbalism and pass through the mushroom rings
and continue on the trail turn to **297.**

259

You quickly manage to reload and fire again, this time the bolt fly's into Falco's heart. The force of your attack sends him back a couple of feet, he gasps for breath and moans right before he removes the shaft from his chest. "I am invincible boy! I am protected by the power of the matron!" He laughs and resumes his attack. You sling your weapon over your shoulder and curse your luck, you realize that your weapons are not going to be able to slay this supernatural opponent. The only option that plays in your mind of overcoming this foe, is by somehow using the spirit stone.

To continue, turn to **51.**

260

Carefully you place the gem back into the socket from whence it came, with a loud click you begin to notice the shimmering changes of the forest around you. You sigh with relief that that was the cause for such strange magic, and you are very pleased that everything was set right.

Turn to **188.**

261

You have weapon drawn and are taking aim at Falco as he charges straight for you. Roll the chance dice.

If you rolled 0-4 turn to **98.**

If you rolled a 5 or higher turn to **147.**

262

You are in utter surprise that these men have appeared in this village, you are unsure if they followed you here? But you witness the leader of the bandits come in the open, he is a tall sinister looking brute with, long black hair, a thin black goatee, a long scar on his left cheek, and has piercing dark eyes. A villager is immediately scooped up in his large hand by the throat, "Where is the outsider? We know he came through here! Tell me at once if you value your life!" The large man growls showing his yellow teeth. The shaken man is too terrified to respond and is immediately slain on site because of it as an example to set fear in these people. "Very well we have other ways of obtaining what we need." The leader barks as he signals his men to begin setting fire to the very inn that you are inside. You must act quickly if you are to escape unnoticed.

If you wish to run out the front door and find safety turn to **247.**

Or if you would rather find an alternate means of escape turn to **349.**

263

You quickly raise your shield, just as the bolt leaves the bow and block the shot. After you have raised your shield the bandit leader has already thrown his bow to the ground and pulled out two ink black daggers and rushes towards you with a loud battle cry. The leader of the bandits is a fearsome opponent, he moves with surprising agility. You attempt to use your shield to block his series of strikes with the two daggers, but after you block the arrow he immediately trips you with a sweep of his left leg. You fall to the ground, and your shield is kicked to the side by his other foot. The bandit leader leaps on top of you, and attempts to stab you with one of his daggers. You block the strike with your weapon, and kick the bandit off of you. He regains his footing and paces around poised to strike, "You think you stand a chance against me boy?" Taunts the man. You smirk accepting the engagement of mortal combat. If you have fought this bandit leader before you may add **2** to your attack, otherwise deduct **3** from your attack rating.

Falco Drifkan Bandit Leader (Dual wielding demon claw daggers)

Attack. 30   **Health points. 28**

Armor class. 4   **Magic points. 0**

Hit : 1d6 +4 Poison damage.

(Every time that Falco has a successful hit, you must roll the chance to determine if you are poisoned. If you roll under a 4 you are poisoned and take an extra **1d4** poison damage every round until you either use a antidote, or curing to cure the condition.)

If you survive the combat turn to **92**.

264

You are taken off the tail and deep inside the forest where no man can go without a tree folk guide to the sacred grove, and it is more splendid and beautiful than you thought it would be. The trees here are not dark, and threatening instead they vary in type, color, and bare all types of seeds, and fruits. Instead of the area seeming dark and closed off, it is vibrant with rainbows and widespread. There are even more tree folk here, around thirty you count. "Welcome to the sacred grove Sabin, only the privileged can venture here." Says Oak Root as he gazes upon his home with pride. "Every guardian is born here, and the secret of the trees are forged here. For eons we have tended this grove, it is the soul of the forest and all life." Adds Leaf Brow as he points to the different types of trees that only grow here. (The magic energy here instantly rejuvenates all of your lost magic points.) "You must try the abyra fruit Sabin." Oak Root states as he picks one of the rainbow colored pear shaped fruits from a smaller tree with a golden colored bark. You graciously take the fruit and sample a bite, its juices are so fruity and energizing that you immediately recover **3** life points. (You may put the rest of the fruit in your back pack and keep it as a meal.)

"Oak Root, how can I find Allendrah?" You ask. The tree folk smiles at you, and bends down closer to your face. "You will need the guardian ring to find the only beings that can get you to Allendrah." Whispers the massive tree folk. You shrug your shoulders, "How might I come by this guardian ring?" The tree folk removes a slender brass ordinary looking ring from one of its branch like arms and slowly hands it to you. (mark this down as a special item. The guardian ring also adds one to chance roll values.) "This is the guardian ring Sabin, it will tell you how to reach Oona!" With a confused expression on your placid face you shrug your shoulders again. "Oona?" You ask in a faint whisper. "Queen of the Fae, escorts to Allendrah. Only the fae can take you to Allendrah, speak her name and she will show you the path." You nod. You wonder why the fae would be the escorts, past rumors of these creatures are they are little pranksters that only delight in causing chaos.

"Young Sabin, and now soon to be hero of the forest. To find the trail again, use the guardian ring. But before you go off into the dangerous of the forest, you may take one of the fruits or nuts that grow in the grove." Oak Root says as he points back to the many trees in the distance. (You may take any of the listed items below, but only one and mark it as a backpack item.)

Abyra fruit - Restores all lost life points to the maximum starting level.

Takra fruit - Reduces the next set of damage taken by 50%.

Ghost Nut - Makes you invisible counts as one use of ability of Invisibility. (Example : if you do not possess the ability of Invisibility the next time you have the option to use the ability you may use it one time without the magic point cost penalty.)

Guardian Nut - The next time you deal damage it is doubled, one time use only!

After you are finished adjust your character sheet properly then turn to **328.**

265

Instinctively you raise your shield as the spider secretes a green fluid from its maw, the second it hit's the shield the green slimy fluid hisses as it melts a hole through your shield. (You must delete your shield from your character sheet, it is useless now.) You drop your shield to the ground with your mouth agape, you are in awe in this creatures many forms offense. It suddenly leaps onto you, knocking you to the ground. You recover quickly and strike it its most vulnerable spot, its eye. The creature squeals before dying on the ground, you rise to your feet and brush off the dirt and forest debris that are stuck to your attire. You are very thankful that your shield protected from such a dangerous attack, you glance down at the floor and see a smoking hole from where the spit of the monster landed. You proceed very cautiously not wanting to run into more of these terrifying oversized spiders. Soon the tunnel you are in forks, there is a tunnel leading upward and one downward.

If you wish to take the tunnel downward turn to **57.**
If you would rather take the tunnel upward turn to **115.**

266

At the cost of **3** magic points you concentrate on your illusion and soon you are completely invisible. You walk out into the open right passed the first two bandits unnoticed, but before you can reach the cover of the next building the spell is already wearing off. "Seize him!" Shouts a bandit from your left as he rushes towards you with weapon in hand. Without a second to spare you run, and suddenly more bandits appear on the scene.

Turn to **6.**

"You have just had the very same vision I have had every night for the last twenty days." Oona's voice states. You turn around and realize that you had slept on a mossy grass patch, and the ferry queen was watching you sleep. "What was that?" You ask confused of your dream like premonition. The tall queen stares into the spirit stone that is still in her hands, "Something terrible. Something we cannot let happen, you have just seen the face of pure evil." You swallow a large lump that appears in your throat, overwhelming dread floods your senses. "You mean what I saw in my vision is going to happen?" You ask in a terrified tone. The ferry queen does not react to your question, "Not if this stone is returned to the elves!" You nod, and then sigh with relief knowing that you will have succeeded in your quest this afternoon. "Who is she?" You ask full of morbid curiosity.

Oona's eyes stare blankly into yours, "You have just seen the Matron of the Damned! Lilith, the mother of demons and all evil." The very name of the demon queen stirs fear in your heart and soul, you have never heard of such a being or even knew that something so dark and evil had existed. "She resides in the Nether hells, the realm of darkness. Banished there by the others of her kind!" Oona adds in a monotone soft voice as if reciting a litany. "Her own kind? Other demons?" You ask full of confusion. Oona shakes her head, "No…She was not always known as the Matron of the Damned, she was once a being of great beauty and kindness. Lilith was once a celestial, the beings that created all life and magic on Lamara." "What happened then?" You ask eagerly listening to the tale. "There were two celestials that existed, and assisted in all creation. Gandohr, and Lilith.

Gandohr was also known as sun god, and Lilith was known as Luna or moon goddess. They created all of the high beings, dragons, elves, and my kind. Gandohr demanded total dominion over Lilith and the entire world, but Lilith did not want to be subservient to Gandohr. She wanted to be equal to him and everything else, but he would not have it. That is when the great unbalance occurred. The two celestials fought over Lamara, and nearly destroyed everything. But the lesser beings of our world convened one evening with the celestials and peacefully suggested that they end their dispute, and share the power they had. Lilith wanted nothing to do with it, she wanted dominion over Lamara and its beings. From that night forward there was a great struggle, and every high being combined their powers to banish Lilith from this plane of existence.

She was banished to world of pain, suffering, a world that molded to her will. She birthed an army of horrible beings called demons. And to make sure that something like this could never happen again, Gandohr declared that he would never interfere with Lamara and its beings again. That is when the other high beings were left in charge of protecting Lamara, and the spirit stone was created in the charge of the elves and then passed to humans worthy of guarding the secrets of magic." Your mouth is agape in fascination in this ancient tale that your ears or any human has not heard in so long.

"However, Lilith cannot return to this realm. She was banished by forces that her evil intent magic cannot stand against?" Oona whispers to herself as she considers the situation more closely. "Why is that?" You ask. "She was banished by Gandohr and the combined power of us all by field of magic that can never weaken, Gandohr was always more powerful than she. He is unable to return to our world also, so this does not make sense?" You are also equally confused by how this is being done? You have never heard of such things and cannot even comprehend most of what

Oona is talking about. "I do not have the answers, but the elves of Allendrah will. Come Sabin, we must leave at once." Oona says full of steadfast enthusiasm.

Turn to **81.**

268

The glamour of the Azart Forest has taken full effect, and you are unable to escape the circles that you have been walking in for hours. Soon madness sets in and you begin to forget what your mission is and where it is you are supposed to go? You spend your last days wandering the forest endlessly in circles until you starve to death.

Your life and quest end here.

269

An unbelievably beautiful ageless looking woman appears from the grotto, unlike her minions she is not tiny in stature. In fact the omnipotent ferry queen is taller than you, her skin is smooth and milky white. There is a white light aura around here, her wings are almost transparent. Her wild green eyes sparkle like an emerald, and her flawless shape drops your mouth. Her hair is like a heavenly rainbow, every visible spectrum of color is apparent in her hair and glows like a luminescent light. Her thin lips purse as she studies you intensely as she somberly floats towards you surrounded by her guards. Her gaze freezes you where you stand, her flute like voice soothes your being. "You are the last of the Riven Clan?" You nod unable to speak from being so overcome with awe. "Allow me to see the spirit stone." Her soft voice echoes throughout your mind. Obediently you hand her the stone, its glow and warmness surprise and shock her at once. "I have not seen this stone in over two hundred years, you seek Allendrah…." "Sabin, I am called Sabin." You interrupt not meaning any disrespect towards this high being. "Indeed you know my name, and so shall it be that I guide you to the sacred realm of the elves." She answers without taking her eyes from the stone that she now holds in her soft hands. "You have ventured far and long Sabin, come rest and have a meal before we set off to Allendrah." She requests with her soft flute like voice. You nod, just now realizing how hungry you really are.

Turn to **59.**

270

You have your weapon ready and stand in a defensive posture, the strange assailant does not appear intimidated by your combat readiness. "Come here boy, let's see if you know how to use that." Taunts the man as he closes in for the battle.

Bandit

Attack. 13	Health points. 16
Armor Class. 2	Magic points. 0

Hit : 1d6+1

You can evade the combat after one round by turning to **83.**

If you win the combat turn to **345.**

272

After you travel downstream to where the current does not appear as dangerous you step into the water and it is much colder than you expected. Suddenly the current slams into you and you lose your footing and are carried further downstream, you attempt to fight the current but you are forced under the water. Panic begins to set in as you fight to surface and breath, but the current is far too strong.

If you possess the ability tolerance and wish to use it turn to **323.**

If you do not possess this ability turn to **93.**

271

With a well placed final blow the final soldier briar arachnid falls over dead, you sigh with your exhausting victory. Sensing that you do not have much time before more arrive, you quickly gather yourself and proceed along the tunnel. Sweat pours from your forehead as you make haste to reach the end of this dreadful place, the humidity is sapping you of your energy. The tunnel seems to turn and wind endlessly but you finally manage to reach a fork in your path, the tunnel splits into two directions. One leading upward, and the other going downward.

If you wish to take the tunnel leading upward turn to **41.**

If you would rather take the tunnel leading downward instead turn to **211.**

273

Despite your odds of surviving this onslaught you focus your minds eye onto the spirit-stone, all of your mental effort is channeled into the lifeless rock. Within an instant before the spider horde is upon you, the stone lights up brightly bathing you a blinding white light. Like a beacon of hope the light becomes so bright you are forced to close your eyes, and the spider army pauses screeching and hissing at the magical force you are holding tightly in your hands. You feel a psychic force and flowing through your mind unlike anything you have ever felt before, for a moment the entire knowledge of the Riven Clan is in your minds eye. A wave of mental power is emanated through you to the spirit stone and then amplified into a torrent of energy that is sent into your enemies ranks. The briar arachnids are sent flying with such force against one another that they are squashed like an accordion, like a ripple in a still pond the wave of energy expands and finishes the rest of your enemies. Jaw agape you stare at your lifeless surroundings astonished by the awesome power of the artifact you possess. The light of the warm rock dims slightly, and the milky white aura that you now bask in rejuvenates you. (Restore all lost health points and magic points to their original totals.) Just as you are about to set off for Allendrah something in the distance catches your eye.

Turn to **241.**

274

The tunnel gets warmer and more humid as you step deeper and deeper underground, a thin layer of water lines the floor as well as a variety of mosses and thick mud. The smell is not pleasant by any means, the odor is similar to a sewer. You do notice that even though the briar and vine growth is natural, something had to have made these networks of tunnels. But who or what? You pray to the spirits that you will not find out. Sweat pours down your face, and your skin is now sticky. The warm air does not help your trek, you feel your energy slowly being sapped from your body. The light from your torch grows smaller and barely flickers from the lack of oxygen in this tunnel, you stop in your tracks when you notice something strange on the walls. At first you are not sure at what you looking at, you notice several large white sacs pulsating. Each of the seven sacs is about as large as your backpack, and they are fused to the lining of thick vines by a silky web like fibers.

If you wish to investigate the pulsating sac's turn to **315.**

If you choose to ignore the strange sacs and continue through the tunnel turn to **27.**

275

Using **2** magic points, you attempt to use the healing nature of your magic to ward off the effects of the orange gas that has now engulfed you, but you only feel the effects of the poison being slowed and not cured. Realizing that the magic will not stave off the symptoms of the gas for long you must make a run to the safety of the other side of the mushroom field. You must roll the chance dice.

If you rolled 0-4 turn to **330.**
If you rolled 5 or higher turn to **105.**

276

After a couple of long unsure hours pass you by, you finally find the trail. Though it appears in the opposite direction that it should have been, you are relieved to have found it again regardless. You decide that it is not wise to leave the trail for any reason, even if it is risky to walk the path.

Turn to **348.**

277

The left tunnel begins to move upward, making it easier to keep your distance from the pursuing threat. The tunnel winds and turns to the point of being unable to tell if you are still heading the right direction, the clicks from the spider host are growing louder. Soon you come to another fork in the tunnels, there is another left tunnel and one going to the right.

If you wish to take the left tunnel turn to **35.**
If you choose the right tunnel instead turn to **124.**

278

You remain completely motionless, holding your breath your only love your eyes in an attempt to see whatever made that awful noise. You cannot see anything around you, but you can hear something large moving around in the distance. Whatever it is that made that noise is getting closer, you can hear its large feet stomping the ground and moving through the bushes. You can hear a low breathing, and detect the faint odor of something wild a smell that you have not smelled before. Suddenly, a very large bear appears before you. It is about seven feet tall, with grizzly dark brown hair and a very large mouth. Equally surprised by your presence it assumes that you are a threat of some kind as it lets out a very deep loud blood curdling roar before it charges at you.

If you wish to run turn to **295.**
If you would rather stand your ground and fight the large bear turn to **30.**

279

Your next bolt sails straight into the spider's head, with a loud thud it tumbles to the ground lifeless. Without hesitation you proceed further along the dark tunnel, it winds and abruptly turns endlessly. It is not long before you notice that the tunnel forks into two different paths, one tunnel leads upward and the other going downward.

If you choose to take the tunnel leading upward turn to **41.**

If you choose the tunnel leading downward turn to **211.**

280

The elder grabs his staff, it is a gnarled walking stick with several bird feathers attached to a string that has been adorned to the tip. Next the elder approaches you with the stone in his hand, "Sabin. I now relinquish my standing as the Lorna guild mage, as the last of the Riven mages you are now the future of our entire practice!" The elder says with his eyes closed and hands you the glowing warm stone, to your surprise the spirit stone does not feel like an ordinary rock. It feels like a vessel of power and life, but just moments after it is placed into your palms the light fades and the milky white color it has now becomes a dull gray color. "What happened?" You ask in alarm. The elder holds your hands firmly, "this is normal for every new replacement. You must figure out how to awaken its power again, it may seem like an ordinary rock but it is still the spirit stone." The elder whispers to you.

"Let your spirit guide you to Allendrah Sabin, the stone is the key. I have taught you all that I know, now the rest is up to you. I will keep them distracted while you escape. Do not look back!" (Mark the spirit stone as a backpack item.) The elder says as he opens the door and runs in the direction you came from. Realizing what he is about to do you attempt to stop him, when he sees you are following him he stops and shoots you a very heated look. "Go Sabin, this is the only way. I am doing my duty, now you need to do yours. Now GO!" The elder shouts as he pushes you away and runs towards the town's thoroughfare. You shed one last tear for your home before turning around and running. After just moments of seeing your mentor leave, you can shouts. Without looking back you run as hard as you can towards the outskirts of your home.

Turn to **130.**

281

Your bolt lands in the center of the foul creature's eye, it screeches and hisses at you loudly before it falls over dead. You waste no time to continue your trek, the tunnel turns and winds endlessly but you do not let the difficulty of this task deter you from reaching your goal. After a short moment you notice that the tunnel splits into two directions just ahead, you can either take the tunnel leading upward or the tunnel going downward.

If you wish to take the tunnel leading upward turn to **41.**

If you choose the tunnel leading downward turn to **211**.

282

Carefully you sneak over to the cover of the thick green bushes just before the spell wears off and you are completely visible again. You did manage not step on any sticks or even draw any attention to yourself, but your only hope now is that you have gone far enough for them to give up and not find you. Patiently you observe as the two gangly creatures chatter amongst themselves before they head off in the opposite direction that you have moved from. You sigh with relief and emerge from your hiding spot, after a brief examination of your surroundings to be sure that the trolls are no longer in the area do you decide to continue your mission.

Turn to **3**.

283

You turn around and run in the other direction, you dare not look back at any threats they may be on your heels. You are unsure of how far back to go, but when you see two tunnels that you did not notice before you decide to take this opportunity to find a alternate means of escaping this place. There is a tunnel leading upward and another leading downward.

If you wish to take the tunnel leading upward turn to **202.**

If you choose the tunnel leading downward turn to **274.**

284

You manage to gain more ground and out speed your enemies, but they have not given up the chase. You watch as Falco remains just twenty feet behind his horsemen, his cold menacing eyes stare at you intensely. The darkness of the night is making it very difficult to navigate efficiently, but you are determined to escape your enemies. You soon realize that the direction you have taken back at the sign may have been a foolish one, just ahead you can see that a very large boulder blocks the path. You bite your lip and shout a curse, you must either turn around or go around the rock and re-locate the path.

If you wish to turn around and take the east path and head for Lark's Bluff turn to **99.**

Or if you would rather go around the boulder and continue your course towards Balsat turn to **342.**

285

A searing white jet of fire flies from your hands and engulfs the two arachnids, they hiss and screech as they scramble to put the violent flames out. The use of this ability has cost you **1** magic point. Just as you assume that the spiders are dead, one of the singed spiders has managed to survive the attack. The angry spider has black smoke flying from its burnt and wounded body, but despite its injuries it leaps at you. You cannot evade this fight.

Wounded Briar Arachnid

Attack. 7   **Health points. 7**
Armor class. 1   **Magic points. 0**

Hit: 1d4+1

(Remember that this creature is weak to fire, incendiary potions and spirit-fire damage is doubled.)

If you survive the combat turn to **61.**

286

Unable to decide how figure out how the mechanism works, you explore the perimeter in hopes of find an alternate way inside. The foundation of the crypt is old, but it is well built to keep grave robbers and intruders from getting inside. The entire crypt was built around solid granite and marble underground, there is no other way inside. You press on past the crypt and leave the cemetery behind.

Turn to **112.**

287

At the cost of **2** magic points you call upon the elemental plane for intervention, you bite your upper lip as Falco closes in for the kill. Just as he is about to reach you, a torrent of wind pulls him making contact with you. You watch as a wind elemental carries him backward and smashes him against a tree violently. You cringe when you hear the sound of his ribs cracking, and then the elemental disappears. This has bought you some time to think. Evil laughter echoes in the forest as the bandit leader rises to his feet, "Is that all you got boy?" Taunts the large seemingly invincible man as he resumes his attack.

If you wish to use a bow/or crossbow turn to **261**.
Of if you would rather use the power of the spirit stone turn to **51**.

288

You narrowly avoid being struck by the first rider's sword, and take this opportunity to dash past the second. They are quick to pursue, and you must find a way to escape them on foot. You force your legs to carry as fast as you can, the shouts from the two bandits in the distance grow louder as they close in. A new solution as presented itself when you notice a steep drop off in the distance, it would be difficult for the enemy to chase you on horses if you can make it there. You can feel your legs burning with exhaustion and your heart is pounding in your chest as you desperately attempt an escape. You barely make it to the ditch, but it is far deeper than you anticipated. You fall and begin to roll violently to the bottom, losing **2** health points. The bandits curse you as the horses stop unable to pursue, if they are going to continue pursuing you they will have to go around the drop off and continue on foot. You slowly get back up and rub the dirt and other debris from your ragged clothing and climb up the other side and begin to run to safety in the Lorna grasslands.

Turn to **36.**

289

You run as fast you can manage with the spider brood on your heels, they are quicker than you thought to expect and more relentless than anything you have ever seen. The small spiders begin to crawl all over the walls and ceilings which allow them to cover more ground than you are able to on the muddy sticky floor of the tunnel. You realize that you must stall them some how if you are to escape.

If you possess the ability spirit-fire and wish to use it turn to **74.**
If you do not possess this ability or would rather use your weapon to stave them off turn to **167.**

290

You use every last ounce of your strength to free yourself from the position you are trapped in, but you are unable to surface before you pass out from lack of fresh air. You are unconscious and drown quickly in the river of the Azart Forest.

Your life and quest end here.

291

Your first shot fells the first soldier briar arachnid, but as you attempt to reload your weapon and take down the second spider it leaps onto. Your bow/crossbow is knocked from your grip, and you are wrestling on the ground trying to gain control of situation as the large black spider attempts to bite you and rip you to pieces with its slashing arms. You kick the spider from you, but before you can draw a weapon to defend yourself the spider is already attack you. You must fight this opponent without a weapon for two rounds of combat.

Soldier Briar Arachnid

Attack. 13   **Health points. 18**
Armor class. 1   **Magic points. 0**

Hit: 1d6 +3

(Remember that this creature is weak to fire, incendiary potions and spirit-fire damage is doubled.)

(You may recover your bow/crossbow after the combat.)

After you have slain your enemy you waste no time to continue down the tunnel, after what seems an eternity of turns you arrive at a fork in the tunnel. One tunnel leads upward, and the other downward.

If you wish to take the tunnel leading upward turn to **41.**

If you prefer to take the tunnel leading downward turn to **211.**

292

You cautiously peek around the corner of the tunnel, and what you see astonishes you. Just ahead you see an eight legged spider-like creature connecting pieces of the briar to thick white webs that it is spraying out of its bulb shaped black and green abdomen. The strangest features of the creature are it seems to be part plant, and has a single large black eye on its green head. The spider creature is about three feet tall and its two front legs have serrated edges on the ends. You observe as it uses its front legs to cut portions of the briar and fuse them to different areas with its silken webbing, it is obviously making a new tunnel and reinforcing this older one. You have never seen such a large spider before, and you are unsure it is hostile or not? You decide that you wish to remain unnoticed and begin to turn around when suddenly it makes a strange clicking noise, and its large inky black single eye stares right at you. You freeze wondering if it can see you, but when it quickly lumbers towards you making an aggressive clicking noise you decide that you must act.

If you have a bow or crossbow and wish to use it turn to **49.**

If you do not possess such weaponry and wish to stand your ground turn to **82.**

If you choose to flee turn to **118.**

293

You force your steed to take the east path to Lark's Bluff, from here the road turns downhill allowing you to gain more and more speed. The pursuing bandits also are using the downhill charge to their advantage, as they begin to close in on you. You keep trying to scan the area ahead for any means of alluding the enemy as they gain more and more ground on you, but nothing has presented itself yet. You need a distraction if you are going to succeed in escaping this threat.

If you have the ability of Spirit-fire and wish to use it turn to **21.**

If you do not have this ability or would rather use Elementalism turn to **337.**

If you do not possess either of these abilities or do not wish to use them turn to **66.**

294

At the cost of **3** magic points, you quickly whisper the ancient words of the spell and you are completely invisible. You smile relieved that the two spiders ahead do not notice or even sense you, but you are not so sure about the third spider approaching from behind. Quietly you step past the two in front just as the third spider appears, they exchange loud clicking noises with one another. After a brief moment you pause while all three spiders pass you by and scramble into the tunnel leading downward. This leaves the tunnel heading upward completely open and threat free. Your spell soon wares off and you are visible again, and you dart for the tunnel.

Turn to **185.**

295

Despite the large bulky size of the large bear it moves much faster than you had hoped it could, its large thick muscles allow it to push its immense size with relentless speed and power. It roars loudly again as it chases you through the brush of the forest gaining more and more ground on you, and you realize that you are not going to able to outrun this bear for long. You must roll the chance dice.

If you rolled 0-3 turn to **16.**
If you rolled 4 or higher turn to **106.**

296

Your reflexes are not quick enough to avoid the arrow that has just struck you in your heart, you only stare at your fatal wound in shock as the bandit leader patiently waits for you to die. With a evil grin on his scarred face, he removes the spirit stone from your backpack. "You lose boy." He gloats as he stands over you as you slowly and painfully die.

You have failed, your life and quest end here !

297

You slowly and cautiously proceed through the trail that is covered in the mushrooms, you are not sure what to expect from this strange cluster of plant life? Even though you attempt to be very careful and not touch the oversized ominous mushrooms, but your shoulder accidentally brushes against one of the sinewy caps. There is a very thin layer of the toxin on your clothes, though it has no effect on you directly you do notice however that all of the mushrooms begin to shake and move. Suddenly the a thick cloud of orange gas begins to spew from the tops of the mushroom caps, jumping back in alarm you try to avoid the strange cloud of poison. But the gas is quick to cover the entire area, and you must act quickly.

If you wish to run back the way you came to avoid the strange poison cloud turn to **8.**

If you possess the special ability of Tolerance and wish to use it to attempt to pass through the mushrooms to safety turn to **47.**

Or if you would rather draw your weapon and start hacking down the mushrooms turn to **87.**

Or if you think it would be more logical to use the ability Elementalism to call upon the wind to carry the gas cloud away turn to **119.**

298

You find yourself starring at something very strange just ahead, an eight-legged spider creature about three feet tall is spinning something into a web like cocoon. The large spider is green and black, with a large black ink colored eye in the middle of its green head. It appears to be part plant, its midsection has several thorns on it as well vine like hairs all over its legs and bulb shaped abdomen. It's two front legs have serrated edges used for cutting and slashing, it also makes loud clicking noises as it finishes its task. You decide to turn around and leave, but after you step on a twig the noise of it cracking attracts the attention of the strange spider-like creature. It clicks loudly and raises its two front legs and charges at you aggressively, you must act quickly.

If you possess a bow or crossbow and wish to use it turn to **49.**

If you do not possess a ranged weapon, and wish to stand your ground turn to **82.**

If you choose to flee instead turn to **118.**

299

Your only options for this situation are to either fight off these fearsome spiders, or turn and flee.

If you choose to fight these creatures turn to **39.**
If you choose to flee, you must roll the chance dice.
If you rolled 0-4 turn to **76.**
If you rolled a 5 or higher turn to **139.**

300

To your horror the farmhouse is ablaze, and the evidence that the enemy was here is too apparent. You quickly run to the property and search for signs of your parents, but see no one in the area. You lower your head in deep sorrow and tears flood your face as you weep for your family. Soon the emotion is replaced by anger and you shout a curse at the this unfortunate day. Before you decide to head back to the thoroughfare you hear a faint shout for help coming from inside the burning building. It is your father that pleads for aid.

If you possess the ability of Elementalism and wish to use to aid you to help your father turn to **44.**

If you do not possess this ability and would rather use the ability tolerance turn to **108.**

If you do not possess either of these abilities or do not wish to use them turn to **215.**

301

Your patience pays off, just seconds when you think that your invisibility cloak is about to wear off the spider-like creatures scurry off out of sight. When you begin to continue your trek the spell has already worn off completely and you are visible once again. You must re-light a new torch, if you do not possess one you must expend **1** magic point to create a light source. The humidity of this tunnel is beginning to drain your strength and slow your progress, and you stop when you notice that the tunnel forks. There is a tunnel leading to the left, and another going right.

If you wish to take the left tunnel turn to **67.**
If you choose the right tunnel instead turn to **175.**

302

At the cost of **3** magic points you slip into the cloak of invisibility, the strange tree like being seems confused and startled by your sudden dissappearance. "Where did you go? What kind of trickery is this?" Barks the massive tree giant searching all over with its glowing green eyes. You say you are standing right in front of it, and with a curious expression on its strange face it slowly reaches one of its branch like arms out and touches you. "Only a Riven clan mage can perform magic such as this, I believe you just make yourself visible again." It booms with its loud voice. Your magic spell wares off and the tree folk is relieved that you are visible again. "I am called Oak Root, the guardian of the Azart Forest. Long have my kin populated the trees of this forest, but still the forest shrinks and continues to die?" Booms the tree folk's loud voice in frustration. You lower your head in sorrow, "I am sorry that man no longer respects the forest, and its beings."

Oak Root smiles at you warmly, "The elves of Allendrah have remained hidden and unseen in their sacred garden for many centuries. Care not for the well being of the forest, I have begged for them to intervene but they never leave the garden to help the forest. I will help as best I can …?" "Sabin!" You say as you interrupt the giant. "Sabin.. I will help you, but you must accompany me to our domain." Beckons Oak Root. "Our Domain?" You ask full of confusion. Oak Root opens his branch like arms wide and it is then that you notice the other tree folk creatures all around you. They all vary in appearance no two of these massive giants look alike. You count at least five others walking closer towards you and Oak Root.

"They have come to see the last of the Riven clan." States Oak Root as he greets his fellow kin. The first of these monsters to look you up and down is just a hair smaller and thinner than Oak Root. "I am Nettle Branch." It says in a softer whispering like voice. "I am called Leaf Brow." Says the second in deep grunt. Leaf Brow is covered in thick large four pointed green leaves, and has only one glowing green eye. "I am Sage Trunk." Says the second largest of these beings. Sage Trunk has a much thicker base and a lighter coloration than the others and speaks with a hoarse echoing tone. You can feel so much magic emanating from these ancient beings, it is enough to make you feel like a tiny insect. "Well descendant of the Riven clan, will you come with us to the sacred grove?" Asks Oak Root.

If you wish to accompany the tree folk to the sacred grove turn to **264.**

If you would rather politely decline their offer and continue your mission turn to **163.**

303

Three large briar arachnids appear on the scene in front of you quickly, and are ready to attack. They are about to launch an assault on you, but your spirit-fire is quicker than they are. With the expense of **1** magic point you fire a steady hissing stream of white fire that illuminates the dark tunnel onto your enemies, they screech and hiss as they are all burnt to cinders. The charred spiders give off a bitter Smokey aroma as they die, you sigh in relief again. You make haste as you jog down the tunnel, you can see spots where sunlight is poking through the briars in the fabricated ceiling. There is a faint breeze of cool air that blows into you, which lets you know that there must a exit close by. With renewed hope that you are about to leave this infernal place behind you pick up your pace and run towards the end of the tunnel. You come to a complete stop though when you notice a briar arachnid dead ahead staring you down, but this spider is different from the others that you have encountered. This one is slightly larger, jet black, and its forearm's are large and oversized. It hisses loudly as it slowly approaches.

If you wish to attack this spider with the ability of Spirit-Fire turn to **19.**

If you would rather attack the spider with your weapon turn to **79.**

If you possess a bow or crossbow and wish to use it turn to **169.**

304

With your weapon ready you charge at the giant monster, it notices your advance but does not appear threatened by your attack. The being is around thirty feet tall, with deep sunken glowing green eyes, and a large wide gaping uneven mouth. After your weapon makes contact with enormous creature it causes little damage, and now the being is aggravated and attacks. (You cannot evade this combat.)

Tree folk

Attack. 20   **Health points. 40**

Armor class. 5   **Magic points. 12**

Hit : 1d10 +4

(This being is weak to Spirit -Fire, as well as fire. Damage dealt with this spell, or incendiary potions is doubled. Every third round of combat the tree folk casts the spell curing and restores **6** health points and costs the being **2** of its twelve magic points.)

If you survive the combat turn to **75.**

305

Your quick reflexes manage to save you from being hit by an acidic green fluid that the spider has secreted from its mouth, you watch as the puddle of green saliva melts the tunnel floor leaving a steaming three inch hole. You are fully prepared when the spider leaps at you from its position, you drop to the ground completely avoiding its attack. You use your weapon to strike the monster in its most vulnerable area, its black cold eye. Your weapon smashes the eye, and green blood sprays from its head like a fountain. The spider screeches and curls up into a ball as it dies slowly. Soon the tunnel forks and you are left with deciding on which to take, there is one going upward and the other leading downward.

If you wish to take the tunnel leading downward turn to **57.**

If you choose the tunnel leading upward turn to **115.**

306

You attempt to run for the door, but you are not quick enough. The four bandits have managed to intercept you before you can get to freedom. You have your weapon ready and fight valiantly, but four bandits is far too many for your level of combat skill to handle and you are eventually overpowered and killed violently. The enemy now has what they sought, the spirit stone of Lamara. You have failed your quest.

Your life and quest end here.

307

You steer your stallion on the path that leads to the right, the remainder of the day is peaceful and relaxing. There are no signs of the bandits in pursuit, you occasionally stop to allow your mount to feed and drink any water you see on the way. Soon though it is dark, you carefully set off the trail to set up a campsite for the night. You are starving you must eat a meal or lose **4** health points. You stare out the star filled sky, and count the constellations that you can find until you succumb to a deep sleep. When you awaken the following morning you restore **2** health points and **1** magic point. You make haste as you put out any signs that you had camped here off the trail and resume your trek, it is another nice summer day. By early afternoon you notice that you have arrived to the opening of a very thick forest, there is a sign just ahead beside a trail that has almost become overgrown with dark green moss. The sign reads:

Azart Forest : Travelers enter at your own peril

You swallow a lump in your throat as you read the sign. As you set foot inside the treacherous wooded forest, a cold sensation runs throughout your entire body. You shiver nervously as you step deeper and deeper into shadows. Suddenly your horse stops and snorts loudly at you, you urge your steed onward, but it will not budge. You grunt in frustration, but decide that you can walk perfectly fine. You hop off your steed and release it from your custody. "You are free, thank you for taking me this far." You whisper and watch the stallion run back towards the Lorna grasslands freely. You slowly turn back around and with a deep breath walk along the moss covered eerie trail of the Azart Forest.

Turn to **146.**

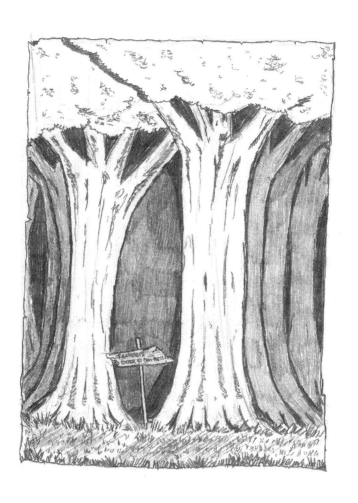

308

You react quickly and are already at a full speed run, with
the trolls charging after you determined to have their meal.
Glancing over your shoulder you see they move more
gracefully than you think their strange anatomy would

allow them too. Their feet are designed to glide over the forest floor with such ease, and it is then that you realize that they are quickly gaining on you. You need a distraction if you are to flee successfully, or you can fight them off.

If you possess the ability Spirit-Fire and wish to use it turn to **20.**

If you do not possess this ability you must prepare for eminent combat by turning to **151.**

309

You raise your shield defensively as the green fluid flies at you, the second that it makes contact with your shield you see smoke and hear a loud hissing noise. You notice that the saliva of this arachnid is acidic, and there is a gaping hole in your shield. (You must discard your shield, it is useless to you now.) As you throw your shield to the ground the spider leaps into the air and attacks you, it screeches as it descends upon you. This fight cannot be avoided.

Briar Arachnid

Attack. 10   **Health points. 13**

Armor class. 1   **Magic points. 0**

Hit: 1d4 +3

If you survive the combat turn to **189.**

310

It does not take very long for you to manage to outrun the enemy, when you notice that you longer are being chased you stop to catch your breath. Your lungs and legs burn from the long exertion, there are no signs of the threat searching you out so you continue walking the path until you find the guild mage's home. You sigh with relief that the bandits have not discovered this hut, for it is a hollowed tree trunk of an ancient tree that was once very abundant long ago.

Turn to **90.**

311

You intensely focus your positive healing energies into the spirit stone, just before the spider mass is about to rend you to pieces where you stand something magnificent happens. The lifeless rock of the spirit stone suddenly trembles in your hand and you are soon covered in a milky white aura as the stone lights up brightly. The overly bright glare of the light forces you to shut your eyes, and makes your spider enemies cower and hiss before the blinding light. A warm sensation flows through your entire body as the re-awakened spirit stone uses the curing energies to protect you with its aura. As the light dims slightly the spiders resume their onslaught and charge into you, cowering in surprise you notice that the second that you become wounded by any of these creatures it is immediately healed as if you were never struck in the first place. Now your fearful expression changes to a delightful grin as you draw your weapon and lash out at your attackers. (You cannot evade this fight, ignore any health points lost in this battle.)

Briar Arachnid Horde

Attack. 40	**Health points. 60**
Armor class. 10	**Magic points. 0**

Hit: 4d20 +10

(Remember these creatures are weak to fire, incendiary potions and spirit-fire damage is doubled.)

After completely destroying the first wave of spiders, the survivor's retreat realizing that you are invincible. After they are all out of sight you sigh with relief and relax to catch your breath, never before have you felt so powerful. The light of the spirit stone dims even more now, and the overwhelming power that once surged freely through your body is drained. You stare into the milky white glow of the legendary artifact with awe, at last you can now find Allendrah. (Restore all lost health points and magic points to their original totals.) Just as you are about to continue through the Azart Forest something catches your eyes.

Turn to **241**.

312

Disregarding the change of the path before you, you continue to walk in the direction that the arrow on the statue had pointed figuring that you would end up in the right place anyway. Hours pass by quickly and you begin to notice that you are traveling in circles, you stumble across your own footprints and you shout your frustration into the evening skies. What does confuse you though is that several pairs of your own tracks end up pointing and heading into different directions, scratching your head you attempt to make sense of what is happening? You try to back track to the owl statue, but you never find it again. You spend the rest of your days wandering lost inside the immense Azart Forest until you run out of food and die of starvation and madness.

Your life and quest end here.

313

As the day quickly begins to pass, you manage to hunt down a rabbit for another meal. By the second day you come across a small village much like yours, the sign at the entrance reads: Kel. The townsfolk appear to be mostly farms and smithies, but keep to themselves. As you walk into the central courtyard no one pays you any attention, in fact you already feel like one of them. You have never been to another village or even this far along the Lorna grasslands, but you decide that it would be a good idea to take shelter here and obtain directions to the Azart Forest. You find the inn quickly and the sign reads : The Field Lodge Inn. To your surprise there is no front door, instead the door frame extra large and wide and the floor is lined with a thick layer of dusty hay. The desk is very large and you notice the innkeeper rustling in the back area that is closed off the public. "We don't get many outsiders here in these parts! You want a room it will cost you three copper a night." The innkeeper's hoarse voice barks. The innkeeper is a middle aged large woman with a scowl on her haggard face. She is wearing a white apron and gray dress underneath.

If you have the three copper and you want to rent a room here for the night turn to **138.**

If you do not have the 3 copper or do not wish to pay for the night and would rather explore the village and obtain more information about the Azart Forest turn to **18.**

∃I4

You strike the final blow on the last arachnid, it screeches loudly before doubling over dead. You wipe the sweat from your brow and do not hesitate to press on, you are in high hopes of escaping this dreadful place. The tunnel starts to slope upward and then wind and turn abruptly before you can see sunlight poking through the ceiling of the tunnel, and you can suddenly feel a slight breeze pushing against you. You are relieved that you are heading towards an exit, and you can see the light ahead of you marking the end of the tunnel. You do however notice another large spider in a few feet ahead, but it is different from the other spiders that you have encountered. This one is a little larger, jet black, and its forearms are far larger in proportion to its body than the smaller of its kin.

If you wish to attack this spider with the ability of Spirit-Fire turn to **19.**

If you would rather attack the spider with your weapon turn to **79.**

If you possess a bow or crossbow and wish to use it turn to **169.**

315

You hold your light over one of the sacs, the movement inside becomes intensified as you study these strange sacs. You can see dozens of little jittery spider like creatures wriggling around inside the sac, you jump back in alarm. Each of the spiders inside are about as large as your palm, and when you decide that it is best for you to move on you can hear a tearing noises and clicking sounds. The sacs are bursting open revealing a horde of tiny hungry baby spiders, and like a wave of ocean current they are attracted to your light and body heat and move towards you. You try to escape the wave of tiny eight legged horrors as they advance like a ravenous flood of rats, but you are surrounded by the spider brood and must fight your way to safety.

Briar Arachnid Brood

Attack. 10   **Health points. 20**
Armor class. 3   **Magic points. 0**

Hit: 1d4

If you survive the combat turn to **14.**

316

After you have slain the wolf, two more large wolf's jump out from behind you snarling and charging for you. You brace yourself for the attack. You cannot evade this combat, you must fight for your life.

Large wolves

Attack. 17   **Health points.** 24

Armor class. 2   **Magic points.** 0

Hit : 2d6 +1

After you have slain the last of the wolves you take a deep breath and compose yourself as you relax. (You can take enough wolf meat for up to 3 meals if you choose.) You continue your daunting task of navigating the Azart Forest, after a couple of uneventful incident free hours pass by something catches your eyes. Beside the edge of the moss covered trail you notice clumps of herbs growing and a merry berry bush on the other side. You recall merry berries being a delicacy and used for pies all over western and central Lamara. The tiny round , red, bulb like berries have are the most delicious fruit in all of Lamara. (You may pick enough for up to 2 meals if you choose.)

If you possess the special ability of Herbalism and wish to use it turn to **2.**

If you do not possess this ability or do not wish to use it turn to **60.**

ЗІ٦

After the use of **2** magic points, you quickly call upon the elemental plane for aid. Just seconds after your plea you notice the ground before your feet trembling slightly, and suddenly a tall well built humanoid shaped clay golem burrows out from the tunnel floor. The two deadly spiders pause at the frightening sight of the creature before them, the golems turns its cold soulless eyes in your direction. "What wizard need?" It asks with a low tone voice. You point to the two spiders just ahead, "kill." You command simply. The golem wastes no time to advance on the arachnids, they both spray jets of their acidic salvia at the golem. Small holes are burnt into the chest of the golem but that does not stop it from crushing your enemies to death, they hiss and frantically attempt to escape their fate but the golem quickly finishes them off. The large muscular being faces you once more, "I go now." It says before it returns to the tunnel that it had came from and the ground returns to normal.

Turn to **61.**

318

You put all distractions aside and press onward towards your goal, and night comes quickly and it is soon pitch black all around you. (If you do not have a torch you must use **1** Magic point to light your way. And start a campfire.) You attempt to make a decent campsite, but the muddy and soggy moss covered forest floor makes that task difficult. You manage to make a bed out a hollowed out tree trunk and rock, it is not comfortable but will be much better than laying on the ground. Sleep comes slowly, but it is not long before your slumber is disturbed by loud noise. You are alarmed to hear a familiar howling noise in the distance, it is dangerously close but you rise from your makeshift bed ready for danger. Starring off into the distance through the blackness of the night, you notice the dreadful glimmer of red eyes all around you. Your pulse quickens as you hear movement from all around you. Suddenly a large gray wolf jumps out of the darkness and into your campsite with its yellow fangs bared growling hungrily.

If you wish to attack the large wolf turn to **38.**
Or if you would prefer to run turn to **158.**

3I9

You release another jet of flames at the cost of another magic point, but your shot misses its target. You curse your luck, and before you can draw your weapon the spider uses its fore arms to slash at your midsection. You jump back avoiding the attack, but your shirt is torn. Next the spider spit's a stream of its acidic salvia at you, again you barely manage to evade the attack. With a loud hiss the spider leaps onto you, knocking you to the ground. You lose **1** health point, as you struggle to fight off this arachnid. (Since you are unarmed your attack rating is at its base value, but after two rounds you will be able to use your weapon.)

Briar Arachnid

Attack. 10	**Health points.**
13	
Armor class. 1	**Magic points. 0**

Hit: 1d4 +3

(Remember these creatures are weak to fire, incendiary potions and spirit fire damage is doubled.)
If you survive the combat turn to **61.**

320

After several short moments the men surround the corners of the tavern, and then the door swings open again. A very large man appears from the entryway, he is very tall, ,muscular, a thin black goatee, and a long scar down his left cheek. This is the most sinister looking man you have ever seen, and you judge by how the bandits avoid eye contact with him that he is the leader. He studies the tavern and everyone inside it very carefully, "We are trying to find someone that is an outsider. Someone that has something we need, I want everyone here to empty their pockets and let my men look through your belongings." The man orders without changing his malevolent grin on his stern face. One of the three other men at a table stands up in alarm and challenges the mans stature. "You can go through my things over my dead body!" Shouts the enraged villager who has obviously had one too many drums of ale. Two of the bandits spring into action and seize the lone rebel easily, the bandit leader walks right up to the man and puts his scarred face close to his. "Perhaps you have not heard of me.., I am called Falco Drifkan..The scourge of Prox. Leader and master of these men that have so easily overpowered you and now have complete sanction of this province." The mans face is suddenly riddled with fear, but is too terrified to say anything. "So that my orders are not misunderstood, anyone that violates my command will gutted like this man before you." Says Falco as he slides his long black curved dagger along the mans throat. You watch in horror as the man bleeds to death quickly. You must figure out a means of escape, they will kill anyone to get what they are after. You must make a run for it while the doorway is clear. Roll the chance dice.

If you rolled 0-4 turn to **306.**
If you rolled 5 or higher turn to **95.**

321

You do not find it difficult to fight these small spiders off, just moments after emerging from the egg sac's you have slain all of them. Wiping the sweat from your brow in smile in victory at your feat, now that you are no longer hindered by the brood of whatever placed these egg sac's here you continue through tunnel. Soon you can here a loud clicking noise, you stop suddenly in your tracks. The noise is coming from just ahead in the tunnel around the corner where it abruptly turns.

If you wish to investigate what is making the noise around the corner turn to **292.**
If you would rather turn back the way you came to avoid any danger turn to **283.**

322

After a deafening second blood chilling roar to stir the silence, your enhanced senses tell you that is a very large bear. The large bear is directly to your left beside a thick bush, it has probably picked up on your scent and judging by the roar it takes your intrusion as a territorial challenge. Bushes nearby begin to part revealing the large animal as it comes bounding towards you with intense speed. The bear must be around seven feet tall with grizzly dark brown

hair, and large ivory white teeth protruding from its gaping maw.

If you wish to flee turn to **295.**

If you possess the ability Spirit-Fire and wish to use it turn to **326.**

If you choose to stand your ground and fight the bear turn to **30.**

323

Using the ability tolerance you force your lungs to hold air longer than they can normally withstand while you force your bodies muscles to fight the current. It is a long hard fight, and the strain on your body is unbearable, but you eventually manage to surface. The air that you are now breathing seems sweeter than ever, but you still have the current to fight. You desperately push your body to its limits and beyond, by the time you reach the safety of the other side you collapse exhausted and drained of energy. The use of this ability has cost you **4** magic points. After you have rested and recovered fully you find the trail and continue your trek.

Turn to **4.**

324

You suddenly recall what Oak Root had mentioned to your when you had visited the sacred grove, he had said that in order to gain the trust of the fae, that you must recite the name of they're queen. Only those worthy of reaching the sacred home of the elves would know the name. You patiently observe as the tiny humanoid creatures flicker and flutter around you and the spirit stone, "How came you by the stone?" A squeaky voice asks in your ear. You quickly explain that it was handed down to you by the last bearer of this sacred vessel, and it is your mission to return it to the elves of Allendrah. The ferries twinkling eyes study you skeptically as they consider your tale, "Then you must know the secret name of our queen, only she can give you what you desire." The voice squeaks into your ear once more.

Knowing the name, to continue turn to **43.**

325

You tread carefully not to be noticed as you return to the thoroughfare, so far you have not seen any signs of the attackers other than the prints and destruction that they have left behind. You pray that they have not found the guild mage, he is the protector of the sacred spirit stone. In the wrong hands there is no telling what kind of havoc could be unleashed, you quickly dart from bush to bush. You bite your lip as you approach the main courtyard and notice that your friends and fellow villagers are rounded up and bound together before the enemy. You count at twenty of these sinister looking men, most on horseback. They are wearing a dark brown studded leather vest, red sashes, leather caps, but the most striking feature of these evil men is the symbol branded on their arms. There is a black dragon tattoo on each mans exposed arm, and they are heavily armed. You force yourself to contain the anger and hate that desperately wants to surface, besides you cannot help your villagers now anyways. You sigh with relief that the guild mage is not among the captured, you decide that he must be hiding in his shack. You must figure out a way to get there without being seen by the enemy. There are two paths that you can take to get there, but each presents a different challenge. You can attempt to take the back alley just ahead , but you must stick to the bushes for cover. Or you can use a special ability to walk right in front of them unnoticed.

If you possess the special ability Invisibility and wish to use it easily walk right in front of the enemy and head to your destination turn to **170.**

If you do not possess this ability or do not wish to use it, and would rather use the back alley as a means of getting to your destination turn to **25.**

326

Extending your hand at the approaching enraged bear as it charges towards you, a thick stream of white fire spews forth from your palm and surges at the bear. Not deterred from its attack, the bear runs right into the fire. You step to out of the way as the flame covered bear barely misses you, and screams out in agony. This attack has cost you **1** magic point, you watch as the large bear falls to the ground and begins roll around in the dirt. Almost immediately the flames are put out, and the air smells of burnt hair and dirt. The bear quickly rises and growls at you angrily before it begins another assault on you, this time you are unable to run and must fight this animal to the death.

Large Bear (wounded)

Attack. 16   **Health points. 25**

Armor class. 3   **Magic points. 0**

Hit : 1d6 +3

If you win the combat turn to **5.**

327

You waste no time to hurry along the tunnel, you tell that you are getting closer to the end of this tunnel and will be back out in the forest. Despite your exhaustion from this awful place, you force your legs to run as fast they will carry you. You glance back over your shoulder and notice that a flood of briar arachnids have just entered the tunnel that you are in and are charging straight for you. You could never survive a fight against such numbers, your intrusion here has provoked the entire nest to attack in one single coordinated strike. You can see the light from the end of the tunnel just ahead, you smile as you quickly reach the end of the tunnel. However you are not out of harms way just yet.

Turn to **187.**

328

You soon regret departing the infinitely serene sacred grove, and the dark shadowy presence of the forest is not as inviting as you had hoped it would be. Not knowing the location of the trail is unsettling, and there is no telling what types of perils await you on your trek to Allendrah. You glance down at the small brass bronze colored ring on your finger, seemingly ordinary you wonder how a ring can guide you to the trail you seek? After you walk several more feet, you notice the branches of the trees moving without the breeze and pointing in the same direction. At first you assume they are more tree folk, but they do not lumber around like the tree folk do. Instead it is only the branches of the trees that are being moved by some unseen magical force, and then it dawns on you that the ring must be doing it to guide you towards the trail. After you follow the direction that the trees point for about an hour you finally find the trail, you smile with relief and also notice that the tree branches return to their normal positions.

Turn to **163.**

329

Traversing the tunnel that leads in the right direction is easier than you had anticipated, the terrain is level and there is very little debris to impede your progress. Almost an hour passes that is uneventful, but you begin to notice by the way these briar's vines that line the tunnel have been created and manipulated by something, but by who or what is unknown? A cold chill runs down your spine, as you suddenly arrive at another fork in the tunnel. The tunnel splits into two more tunnels, one that goes downward and the other upward.

If you wish to take the tunnel going upwards turn to **202.**

If you choose the tunnel leading downward turn to **274.**

If you possess the ability of Enhanced- Senses and wish to use them turn to **344.**

330

As you are running towards safety, the gas cloud becomes so thick and so overwhelming that you are unable to see clearly. You cannot hold your breath any longer, and as you try to feel your way to safety the mushrooms sticky sinewy poison is all over one of your hands. After you have taken a deep breath of the gas, and the poison on your hand makes your entire arm numb you collapse to the ground unable to move. You desperately try to move your legs and arms, but the effects of the gas put you into a deep sleep in which you will never awaken from.

You have become another victim of the many perils of the Azart Forest, your life and quest end here!

331

You take one deep breath and then shout as loudly as you can as you run towards the mounted bandits full speed. The bandits seem more surprised by the charge then the horses do, and they immediately draw their weapons and prepare to attack. You cannot evade the combat and must fight them as one enemy. (deduct 2 points from your attack rating due to the riders being on horseback.)

Bandit horsemen

Attack . 25 **Health points. 30**
Armor Class. 4 **Magic points. 0**

Hit : 2d6 +2

If you survive the combat turn to **72.**

332

You turn and run as fast you can go, the troll duo is upon as quickly as you are visible to them. They shout and snarl at you as they pursue, your legs quickly burn with exhaustion as you try to shake these marauding monsters. They are far quicker than you had expected them to be, and it is your unfortunate luck that as you glance over your shoulder you do not notice a loose rock just ahead and trip over it. You roll and crash onto the forest floor, and this buy's the trolls enough time to close the gap between you and them. You are struck upside the head by a club like weapon, and you are unconscious immediately. Your life ends quickly, and you do not feel the pain of the two trolls beating you to death.

Your life and quest end here tragically in the Azart Forest !

333

You tread westward without the ease of a trail, since there is a peculiar enchantment cast over the forest basic navigation skills will not work. You will only have your abilities and instincts to guide you, and you have gone too far to fail now. You notice that you cannot travel as quickly because off all the rocks and sudden steep levels of the forest floor, but you continue west anyway. After the rain finally ends, do you pause to dry your clothes and make yourself more comfortable. Right before you grab your backpack to continue, a strange aroma fills your nostrils and grabs your curiosity. You can faintly smell something being cooked just ahead, you wonder if you are the only traveler here or if someone else has made a campsite and is now cooking meat. The smell is delicious and inviting, but you do not know who or what is preparing the main course.

If you wish to investigate the location of the smell turn to **85.**

If you would rather ignore the odor and continue your course turn to **318.**

334

At the cost of **2** magic points you chant a plea to the elemental plain for assistance, your concentration is broken just as you finish your incantation by the arrival of four briar arachnids. They hiss and click loudly as they determine you are a threat, and just as you prepare for an emanate attack something happens that brings you a long sigh of relief. Suddenly a loud crashing noise makes you step back just as the hulking gray figure of a clay elemental breaks through the tunnel wall. A six foot heavily built man like golem stands between you and the slashing fore arms of four fearsome large spiders. "What does young mage desire?" Grumbles the low tone of the golem's voice. You point your index finger at the arachnids, "Kill!" You command as simply as and direct as possible. The large golem nods and as the spiders attempt to leap at you the heavy golem slams into all four of them with its weight, one is smashed and killed quickly but the other three attempt to fight back. You observe as the elemental guardian grabs one briar arachnid and rips its head off completely and smashes its body into another of its kin, and the last spider squeals and retreats out of sight. The golem turns and faces you, its glowing orange eyes show no signs of fatigue or thought. "I go now, monsters gone." It grumbles as it suddenly crumbles into chucks of dried clay. You thank the elementals for their aid, and then you continue down the tunnel.

turn to **86.**

335

You run for it as fast and hard as you can, it does not take long for the bandits in the area to notice your escape attempt. They shout amongst themselves to capture you, suddenly two bandits appear before you, there is no way around them you must fight them. (This combat will only last two rounds.)

Bandits

Attack. 25   **Health points. 28**
Armor class. 3   **Magic points. 0**

Hit : 2d6 +2

After the two rounds of combat you manage to buy enough time to slip past these two and proceed with your escape.

Turn to **6.**

336

In your last moments of desperation trying to awaken the powers of the spirit stone, the spider swarm is upon you. You are quickly maimed by the army of spiders, and torn to pieces where you stand. Shortly after your gruesome demise, the powerless rock of the spirit stone is forced from your lifeless fingers by a sinister figure. This day on will be remembered as the day a great and all powerful evil was unleashed upon Lamara.

You have failed your quest !

337

At the cost of **2** magic points you silently chant to the elemental plane for aid, and almost immediately there is a response. You can see from the corner of your eyes as the ground behind you moves, and two clay limbs appear from the trail and grab one of the bandit horsemen from his steed. The man shouts as he is forced into the granite below and crushed to death by the force of the unnatural spell. His comrade stops to try to help his friend, but Falco slams past his mercenaries and continues the chase without aid. You had hoped that your spell would have foiled all of the bandits, but it has left you alone with the leader who is rapidly gaining on you. Falco appears on your right side, he has his sword drawn and swings at your face. With lightning quick reflexes you react without thinking and dodge the attack, and as his vulnerable side is open to you, you use your leg to kick him from his stallion. The bandit leader topples over off his horse cursing you on the way to the ground. You smile at your victory and escape, you do keep riding hard and fast until the bandits are completely out of sight.

Turn to **174.**

338

You back track until you reach the fork in the tunnels, and decide to take the tunnel leading downward. You notice immediately that this tunnel is far different than the other, the further downward it goes the humidity becomes more and more unbearable. Sweat pours down your face, and thin pools of water and thick mud with rotted forest floor debris makes walking around difficult. It is also very dark and you must use a torch to light your way, (If you do not possess a torch you must expend **1** magic point to create a light source if you have not already.) It isn't long before you reach a large chamber with strange large pulsating white sac's are covering the walls, and there is a musky odor that is heavy in this room also.

Turn to **315.**

339

After about an hour everyone's attention is directed to the tavern door as it violently swings open, and four ruffian men enter the bar with weapons drawn. To your horror the second you notice the black dragon tattoo's on the shoulders your jaw drops, you figure that they must have been able to track you from home to this village. You must act quickly if you are to escape and reach the Azart Forest.

If you wish to make a run for the doorway turn to **306.**

If you possess the ability of Invisibility and wish to use it to escape turn to **233.**

If you do not possess this ability or do not wish to use it and would rather wait and see what is going to happen first turn to **320.**

340

You run as hard as your legs allow you to, and you are immediately noticed by the two hungry trolls. "Over there Ock! Get him." Shouts one of the trolls as it begins to pursue. The second troll hops out of a nearby bush right behind you and is on your heels, they are far quicker afoot than you had hoped they would be. Soon you go crashing to the ground after you trip on a loose rock that you did not see, and with a loud joyful shout the troll that was behind you jumps on top of you. Its warm batted fowl breath is on your face as it drools all over your shirt, "now we eat." It huffs as it takes a club like weapon and strikes you in the head with it. You are unconscious immediate, and it is fortunate that you are unable to feel them tear you to pieces for cooking and eat you.

Your life and quest end here.

341

Despite your magical energies being completely drained, you attempt to awaken the stone by an alternate means. You cringe as the spider host is almost upon you, but you do not give up hope for any kind of intervention. You force your very life-force into the stone, and what little strength you possess causes something very strange to happen? You begin to feel light headed and very weak, but you also notice that the spirit stone suddenly begins to tremble in your hands as a milky white light appears from it. You feel a surge of power unlike anything that you have ever felt before flowing through your body, in an instant the wisdom and power of the Riven clan are one with you and your mind. A blinding white light flashes all around you, the attacking spider horde pauses hissing at the awakened might of the legendary spirit stone. The light grows so intense that you are forced to shut your eyes, the spiders seem reluctant to advance now and soon begin to slowly retreat. The spirit stone sends a warm soothing sensation throughout your entire body, (Restore all lost Health points and magic points to their original totals.) The aura and bright light of the spirit stone dim slightly and you open your eyes, the spiders all have retreated to the safety of the nest inside the oversized thorn bush structure. You sigh with relief, you have just narrowly escaped a gruesome fate. Just as you are about to set off for Allendrah, something strange grabs your attention in the distance.

Turn to **241.**

342

You quickly turn and run, and the man is quick to chase you. Despite the armor and everything this man is carrying he moves quickly, you force your legs to move in desperation to escape. Soon you can hear more shouting as more of these men appear to help capture you. You curse your luck and desperately attempt to outrun the enemy. Roll the chance dice.

If you rolled 0-4 turn to **190.**
If you rolled 5 or higher turn to **310.**

343

You charge down the tunnel, the clicks and shrieks from the arachnids behind you keeps you motivated not to slow your pace. The tunnel relentlessly turns and winds to the point that you feel like you are going to in circles, but you are relieved to see that sunlight is poking though the ceiling and a gentle breeze blows past you. There is light at the end of this tunnel, your hopes for escaping are ignited. But there is also something just ahead that dashes your hopes of an easy escape, there is a large briar arachnid ahead at the exit. This one though, is different than the others. This spider is jet black, slightly larger, and its fore arms are overly large for its body. It's large eye is focused on you, it lets out a chilling shriek as you approach.

If you have a bow or crossbow and wish to use it turn to **46.**

If you would rather use Spirit-Fire turn to **127.**

If you do not possess a bow or crossbow, or even the ability of Spirit-Fire turn to **207.**

344

You calm your nerves as you rely on your five enhanced senses detect anything of any danger from the two different eerie tunnels. Your senses tell you that there is more danger in the tunnel leading downward than there is the tunnel going upward. You are not too surprised that danger lurks in either tunnel, but your safest choice is to take the tunnel going upward.

If you wish to take the tunnel going upward turn to **202.**

If you would rather take the tunnel going downward turn to **274.**

345

The bandit falls to the ground dead at your feet, you search the body in hopes of finding a clue as to why they are attacking your home. You find five copper coins, a dagger, his leather vest which you can wear (Remember if the vest is equipped it adds one to your armor class.) And you may keep his sword if you wish (Refer to the game rules for #6 for the weapon bonus details.) You quickly hide the body behind a crate and continue through the alley way until you arrive at the guild mage's home, it is a hallowed out ancient tree trunk. You are relieved that the enemy has not discovered this location, for it does not resemble a normal housing structure.

Turn to **90.**

346

You slowly and cautious take the stairs to the next room of the crypt, the chamber is roughly the same size as the one above it. The smell of death and decay floods your senses and you begin to feel very nauseous, the light source that you had noticed from the first chamber is coming from a pit in the center of the chamber. A strong fire burns inside the pit, for how long this blaze has existed you do not know but it lights the entire room completely revealing more writings on the walls. You notice several skeletal remains on the floor, and judging by the tattered remains of the clothing you assume they were grave robbers. You do not see any signs of treasure or anything of importance inside this chamber that would be worth protecting? You wonder if there was a crafty grave robber that succeeded in obtaining the treasure that your ancestors had been protecting, but that theory does not make any sense because the only way one could access this chamber would have to know how to cast spirit-fire and only Riven clan members can perform such an act. You scratch your head in confusion to how these men could have entered this chamber? They were not riven magi at all, they were common thieves. You pace around the chamber looking for anything out of the ordinary, but you see nothing worthy of extra attention?

If you wish to examine the corpses that lie on the floor turn to **54.**

If you would rather leave the unknown perils of the crypt turn to **121.**

∃Ϥ˥

As you begin to cut the rope that has you snared upside down with your weapon, one of the trolls see's your escape attempt and reaches for you. Instinctively you slash at the monster as its large dirty hand stretches for you, the second your weapon makes contact with its rough green coarse skin purple blood oozes from the wound you inflict on its arm. "Get its weapon Ock!" Shouts the troll as it holds its wounded arm. The second troll lifts a club like weapon in its long arm, the strange weapon is part of a tree trunk. You do not have much time to free yourself, you must roll the chance dice.

If you rolled 0-4 turn to **88.**
If you rolled 5 or higher turn to **184.**

348

You proceed onward, after a couple of long quiet unsettling hours you notice that the forest has grown more grim. The trees now have an almost black color to them, the shadows on the ground move from side to side. The moss that covers the ground is a dark brown color, and you can see the black silhouette of crows on branches with red dot like eyes starring at you. You feel like everything in the forest is watching you, and you cannot even trust your own shadow. It is soon very dark, and you prepare a torch from a thick branch that had fallen off one of the trees.

You finally find an ideal location to set up a campsite for the night, you must eat one meal of lose **4** health points. After you have eaten your fill, you wrap yourself in your garments and fall asleep. You are awoken a couple of hours later by loud howling, you cautiously study your surroundings in preparation for an attack, but luckily you are not disturbed and you fall back asleep for the rest of the night. You awaken the next morning restoring **3** health points and **1** magic point. You notice that the sun does not fill the sky today, instead dark gray clouds fill the sky and fill your nerves with uneasiness.

Turn to **34.**

349

You quickly search for another doorway to escape before the building will be ablaze, but you cannot find one. You have to do something and fast, or the enemy will be on you. You can soon smell smoke, and hear screaming from outside.

You run down to the other side of the hallway ahead and open one of the doors to the rooms on the other side of the Inn from where your room is. This one has a single window, this is your best chance of escape is out the window. You break the glass and leap from the from the window to the ground, the impact deals **1d4** damage to you. You quickly run to the next building, suddenly you hear a shout from behind. "We got one trying to run Lord Falco!" You glance over your shoulder and notice the bandit leader standing next to his men with a long bow in his hands, and an arrow is notched and ready to fire.

If you possess a shield turn to **78.**

If you do not or do not wish to use it instead roll the chance dice.

If you rolled 0-4 turn to **134.**

If you rolled 5 or higher turn to **203.**

350

"You truly are a Riven Magi." Oona's voice whispers to you from behind. You turn around just as she and her escort blink back into visibility, she stares at the lifeless body of Falco with disgust. "I had not known that such dark magic was possible, the matron's powers have grown to unimaginable feats. Only you with the power of the spirit stone would have been able to overcome such an opponent. We would not have been able to stand against the weapons that that man was using, they were forged and crafted from the Nether hells. They were designed for slaying beings like us, we truly are dealing with forces that are disturbing the balance of this world." She adds with a hint of fear in her tone.

"Come Sabin, Allendrah is near. We must make haste for the council of the elves, they will have the answers we seek." You follow Oona and her guards deeper into the shadows of the forest. Soon the ferry queen comes to an abrupt halt, you too stop and glance around at your surroundings for anything out of the ordinary. You notice nothing worthy of additional attention, you patiently observe as Oona raises her hand towards a large tree and closes her eyes. You can sense she is using her magic to uncover something in the distance, the trees surrounding you shimmer and the scene changes all together. An opening appears revealing an enormous tree in an open field, this tree is far larger than any other in this enormous forest. It is hundreds of feet tall, and at the tip is a very large bulbous flower like bud that touches the clouds. "Behold, Allendrah Sabin. This is the tree of life, it is the heart that beats in all of Lamara. This tree is Allendrah fortress of the elves." States Oona as she too gazes upon the sacred tree in awe, you look upon the large branches and notice the treetop housing structures.

Small huts and ladders as well as many series of bridges like the canopy of this mythic tree. Of everything you have seen that has shocked you in this forest, none compare to this sight. At the base of the tree is a large golden archway revealing entry to Allendrah. You follow the fae into the enormous infrastructure, and you come face to face with the first elf that you have ever seen. The lone elf is a head taller than you with long smooth silver braided hair, almost femine features in the face. Blue sapphire like eyes study you inquisitively, he wears a long white robe, with golden symbols sewn along the hem. "Greetings Oona, it has been many ages since your last visit." The elf says in a soft peaceful tone and smile on his long face. Oona returns the smile, "greetings Hofta. It has been too long since my last visit, but we come with most urgent news and request council with king Marius." The tall elf seems alarmed by your presence by Oona's distress. "We have a quest…, a human?" He replies in surprise.

"The last of the Riven." Adds Oona. The elf stares at you with awe, "welcome to Allendrah. Last descendant of the Riven, come we will convene with Marius at once." You and the fae follow the elf along a series of stairs high into the tree of life, the other elves only stare at you as if they have never seen anyone like you before. They all look very similar in appearance which seems unusual to you, but they appear to be peaceful and accepting of your presence. At last you are led into a large hut like tower with silver and gold arches, the throne room is beautiful there are statues of different beings and creatures along the rounded walls. There is a large oaken table with seven seats, and the tallest sit's the most decorated of all the elves. The elf king is the tallest of his people, with a long white beard, a golden leaf shaped crown, and is wearing a long green and red robe.

His gray azure eyes study you and Oona carefully as you both slowly approach the royal chamber. "My king, I present Oona and the last of the Riven. They seek council." Hofta confidently reports just as the king and his royal advisors about to ask about the sudden intrusion. Oona steps forward and bows to the mighty elf king who patiently awaits the urgent news, "Your majesty. We have come because there is about to be a breach from the Matron, an event is taking place as we speak." The king nods, "Of course. We are discussing the disturbance that is sweeping the land, we have only just felt it." You and Oona exchange confused looks, "we have brought the spirit stone." She adds. The kings eye's light up with excitement, and Oona ushers you to remove the stone from your pack. "What is your name human?" Demands the king as he slowly steps towards you.

You tell him your name and explain what has happened to you and your family, and also of your quest through the Azart Forest to find this place. The entire room is silent as the elves carefully listen the details of your travels, and about the bandits and their leader Falco. "Fear not! For the Lilith and her minions cannot cross into Lamara. It is impossible, it was only her influence through a complicated ritual that allowed this Falco to possess such unnatural power." Confidently states the king as he surverys the stone that you hold in your hand. "Now, Sabin let me see the stone." You obediently place the stone in the kings embrace, his face lights up as he studies the white stone carefully. "Thank you for bringing it back to its home, you have fulfilled the Riven prophecy." You stare up at the tall elf king with confusion. "What prophecy?" You ask. A wide smile covers the old king's face, "The stone was placed in the Riven clans charge not only as mans link to the field of magic, but upon its return marks a special event. In Lamara's greatest need, one will be selected to do what we cannot."

Still confused you glance over at Oona who is also confused. "What do you mean?" You ask. "All of the high races are forbidden to interfere with the shaping and development of this world, we can only influence its inhabitants. The elves, fae, and treefolk are unable to leave the forest. If we do we lose our power, and will become mortal! The dragons cannot leave their mountains either, because of the umbalance that almost destroyed everthing so long ago Lamara's inhabitants are destined to defend it when necessary.

Through random fate amongst the Riven certain individuals are tested then selected to defend our world from any threat." A lump appears in your throat as you slowly gain an underatanding of what you are being told, "No ordinary man could ever reach our sacred home. Only a true Riven clan member can do what you have done Sabin." States the king in a very serious tone as his eyes stare into you. The other elves at the large council chamber break into discussion ignoring you and Oona completely, the distress and unrest in the room makes you nervous. "Silence my people, there is much to discuss in due time. We have guests and must see to it that Sabin and Oona are well taken care of." Instructs the king as he stares down everyone in the great throne room. "For now Sabin, eat, and rest. Your real quest has only just begun!" Lectures the king as he prepares to leave the room. Your hopes of your long journey ending with Allendrah are no more. It would appear that fate has other plans for you. Should you accept the next adventure it will further chronicled in part two of the Dragon Lore series entitled:

Voyage of the Cursed Sea